ELLE GRAY | K.S. GRAY

OLIVIA KNIGHT
FBI MYSTERY THRILLER

FATAL GAMES

Fatal Games
Copyright © 2023 by Elle Gray | K.S. Gray

All rights reserved. Without limiting the rights under copyright reserved above, no part of this publication may be reproduced, stored in or intro-duced into retrieval system, or transmitted, in any form, or by any means (electronic, mechanical, photocopying, recording, or otherwise) without the prior written permission of both the copyright owner and the above publisher of this book.

This is a work of fiction. Names, characters, places, brands, media, and in-cidents are either the products of the author's imagination or are used fic-titiously. The author acknowledges the trademarked status and trademark owners of various products referenced in this work of fiction, which have been used without permission. The publication/use of these trademarks is not authorized, associated with, or sponsored by the trademark owners.

CHAPTER ONE

"**B**ROCK, ARE YOU THERE? I CAN'T SEE YOU!"

There was screaming in the background of the call, and Yara's face was stricken with terror. She frantically searched for Brock's face, the screen crackling a little indicating the signal was bad.

"Yes, we're here. What the hell is going on, Yara? Are you on the plane?"

There was a delay in Yara's reply as the screen shifted and went static. But then her face returned, and she looked even more terrified than before.

"I'm on the plane," Yara confirmed. "But I think something's wrong. The plane is going down."

"What? Yara!" Olivia blurted. But it was too late. After another scream from Yara, the call was cut short, and Olivia's heart plummeted into her stomach.

Brock immediately tried to call her back, but this time, there was no response. He ran a hand through his hair, clearly terrified. How could he not be? One of his closest friends was in a plane that was quickly plummeting to the ground. There was no way she'd make it out alive.

"What do we do?" he asked, turning to Olivia. She fumbled for words, but for once, she didn't have a solution. What were they supposed to do? Yara's plane was going down somewhere in the middle of nowhere. They didn't even know exactly where she was going. Olivia knew how unlikely it was that anyone would survive the crash, but they had to try something—if only for their own sanity. She knew Brock couldn't just accept what they'd seen before their very eyes.

"We'll, um, we'll make some calls. See if we can get a fix on the location of the plane. Which airport did Yara fly out of?"

"I… I don't know. LAX, I guess? But it could've been anywhere. I wasn't paying attention. I should've been paying attention."

Olivia guided Brock to a seat. "Breathe. You need to breathe. I'll see what I can do."

Her heart raced as she tried to find a way to call the airport. She didn't want to just sit there and wait on hold with customer service, and she couldn't exactly drive down there herself; so all she could do was try to get through to air traffic control or security and hope for the best.

"How can I help you?" an operator answered on Olivia's third ring.

"I'm Special Agent Olivia Knight with the FBI. I need to be transferred to operations," she said.

"And what's this regarding?"

Olivia bit back the scathing reply on her tongue. The woman was just doing her job. She didn't know that the lives of Yara and dozens of others were at stake.

"I've just received a call from a passenger onboard a flight. The plane is going down, and they need urgent assistance."

"Are you sure?"

"Yes, I'm sure. The passenger was certain of it."

"Do you have the flight number?"

"No. It was a private jet. There weren't many people on board. It was headed to… I don't know where it was headed. Somewhere in the mountains…"

"Ma'am, are you being serious?"

Olivia bristled again. "I'm dead serious. My friend called and said the plane is going down. We were cut off from her—there were people screaming. I'm a damn FBI agent! Of course, I'm serious!"

"Yes, ma'am, I'm sorry."

Olivia hated to bite the woman's head off like that, but it had to be done. She was placed on hold and transferred over to operations where a harried-sounding man picked up. Olivia was a little calmer and explained the situation as quickly and concisely as possible.

"There were several private flights that departed this evening. Do you at least know what time the flight took off?"

"I… I think it was around six in the evening your time. And the passenger's name was Yara Montague, if that helps."

"It does. Give me one moment."

Olivia held her breath as the man typed away on a keyboard, the click-clacking of the keys putting Olivia even more on edge. She knew that he was trying his best to help, but nothing felt like enough to soothe her frayed nerves. She glanced at Brock and saw that he had his head in his hands. Now wasn't the time for him to fall apart on her, but she had no way to stop it. If he was going to spiral, then she'd have to be strong for both of them. She took a deep breath and tried to stay calm. That was the least she could do.

"The flight in question… we've lost GPS signaling. You're right; there's something wrong with the plane," he said. "It looks like they've gone totally off the map… but their location disappeared over twenty minutes ago. I'll alert the necessary—"

"So, you don't know where the plane is? Not at all?"

"Well, according to the flight path, it should be on its way to Colorado, but the signal we received from the plane was going in a different direction. Straight across the Pacific. I don't know how this wasn't picked up on sooner. Bear with me—I'm doing everything I can to find out what's happening."

Olivia's stomach somersaulted. What on earth was going on? If the plane wasn't even flying in the right direction, then what had the pilot been doing? Perhaps he'd been intoxicated and didn't know what he was doing. Or maybe he was deliberately going off course, but Olivia had no idea why that would be. Why fly across the ocean if they were supposed to go to Colorado? Whatever the scenario, he'd likely doomed Yara and the other passengers to death.

"I need to know where that flight is going."

"Ma'am, I'm going to have to let you go. I'm sorry. I'll return your call when I have answers. Lives are likely at stake here. This needs my full attention."

"But—"

Before Olivia could say anything more, the man hung up on her. She let out a frustrated cry, tempted to throw her phone across the room. But one glance at Brock reminded her to keep it together. Losing her cool wouldn't help anyone.

"She said the plane was going down," Brock whispered. "In the middle of the ocean… there's no chance she's surviving that, Olivia. No chance at all."

Olivia knew it was likely true. Not even the most expensive private jets could survive crashing into the choppy ocean waters. But Olivia couldn't admit that out loud. Not when Brock's face was already stricken with grief. She rushed to him and put her arms around him, holding him close to her.

"Don't give up. We never give up," Olivia murmured. "The officer will call back when he knows more. He said the flight was on an unusual path, not the one that was planned. I think there's more to this. Pilots don't just veer off in a different direction."

"What are you saying?"

Olivia swallowed. "I don't know what I'm saying. But I don't think we've heard the end of this. I think there's something bigger going on."

"You're not making any sense…"

"Do I ever?" Olivia said, a half-hearted attempt at a joke. "We know from experience that crazy things happen every day. Crazier things than people surviving a plane crash. Maybe they just hit heavy turbulence. Maybe by changing their flight path, they found somewhere safer to crash land. There could've been an issue on the plane that required an emergency landing… we don't know. We can't begin to speculate. We'll just have to sit tight and hope for the best, won't we?"

Brock didn't look the slightest bit convinced by Olivia's pep talk, but he said nothing more on the matter. They sat there for a long time, trying to hold themselves together. Olivia tried to make more calls to find out what was going on, but it soon became clear that no one had the time to talk to her about it when they were working hard to find the plane. Instead, she resigned herself to making sure Brock was okay. She knew all too well how uncertainty could break a person down. She had to be there for him while he muddled through the anxiety and the pain.

All the while, Olivia had to sit in the hurt of losing a new friend. She hadn't known Yara for very long, but she cared for her anyway. After everything the actress had been through with her addiction, it seemed so cruel that life was being stolen from her now. She was finally on the path to recovery, and now even that might've been snatched from her. If she even survived this ordeal, would she be able to keep that up? Olivia closed her eyes and prayed for a different ending to the story. She prayed Yara would make it out alive.

And that's when she heard the phone ringing.

Brock didn't look up at the sound of his dial tone, lost somewhere in his grief, but Olivia's eyes widened when she saw the caller ID.

"Brock… it's her. It's Yara calling!"

Brock snapped out of his daze, staring for a moment at the phone. Olivia felt a surge of hope, but it was shortly followed by a sickening suspicion that something was wrong. As Brock picked up the video call, Olivia waited to see Yara's face appear on the screen.

But it wasn't her face that greeted them. A golden mask stared back at them, the rest of the person's face obscured by a hood. In the background of the video, Olivia could see Yara lying unconscious. Her forehead appeared to be bleeding, her skin was covered in grease and soot, and she was lying on golden sand. Olivia shook her head in disbelief. Where were they? What had happened to her?

The person behind the golden mask chuckled, their true voice disguised by a voice changer. Strangely, the voice was deep and raspy, but they still couldn't tell if it was a male's or female's. Olivia felt a chill race down her spine. Suddenly, none of this felt like an accident.

The person stared them down from behind their strange mask, still chuckling to themselves.

"Hello, Brock Tanner. Hello Olivia Knight. Did you come to play?"

CHAPTER TWO

"WHAT THE HELL IS THIS?" BROCK DEMANDED, glaring at the screen. The person in the gold mask laughed yet again. Whoever they were, they were terrifying. Their eyes blazed blue behind the golden mask.

"It's a game, Brock. Isn't all of life a game, after all?"

Brock's nose flared, and he squeezed the phone so hard it nearly shattered in his hand. "I don't have time for whatever you're trying to pull. This is ridiculous. What have you done to Yara?"

"Nothing that wasn't necessary for a little bit of fun. She's part of the game, too, you see. Perhaps an unwilling player, but part of the game nonetheless. She'll start having fun soon, I assure you."

"Stop talking like this and cut to the chase," Olivia said sharply. "Who are you, and what do you want? What happened on the plane? Were you a passenger? Did you make it happen?"

The person in the gold mask sighed. "Fine. It seems clear you don't want to have any fun with this. So, I'll tell you how it is. The plane went down, yes, but it was no accident. I had it planned long before those people ever boarded the flight. And when it went down, I knew it wouldn't crash, but we allowed the passengers to *believe* that the plane was going down for good."

"You're sick," Olivia seethed.

"What can I say? It put on a good show for the audience."

That made her recoil in horror. "The… audience?"

"Yes, dear Olivia. The audience. Every move I make is livestreamed across the world. I've got thousands of viewers who follow my every move—who seek the delights of life. *Real* life, unbound by the constraints of normalcy and full of the ragged edge of infinite possibility!"

Brock looked over at Olivia. This person was crazy. What had they gotten into now?

"It seems you haven't heard of me… they call me the Gamemaster. It's my job to entertain the masses. For the past three years, I've been setting challenges—tasks for those who wish to live a true life. For money, for fame, for certain rewards… and now, after three long years, this is my most ambitious one yet. It's also my most controversial. I guess I'm going to get some flak for this… but oh well. I live to entertain, not to people please. And now, I am excited to extend my invitation to both of you! I'd like you to play along."

"With what?" Brock roared. "Pretending to crash on a desert island? Playing with people's emotions? You're insane!"

"Far from it, Mr. Tanner. I am merely seeking to push you—to push *everyone*—to the limits of what they believe can be done and then break through them like glass. Fear and bliss! Terror and joy! Can't you feel it?" The Gamemaster's eyes flashed in ecstasy behind the mask. "And I don't think you're going to refuse my offer to join in… considering there will be lives at stake."

FATAL GAMES

Olivia's heart dropped to her stomach. "What is that supposed to mean?"

"It means, Ms. Knight, that not all games are fair. If you refuse to join me, then I'll kill every single contestant on this island before they even have a chance to figure out what's happened to them. If you bring your FBI friends in to save the day, I'll kill them too. And since this is for entertainment, it won't be quick, and it won't be pretty. You don't want to see Yara's pretty head on a spike now, do you? That won't be very fun for her fans, now, will it?"

Brock trembled with rage. "You wouldn't!"

"I would. Because if you're not willing to cooperate, I won't hesitate to do some awful things—things you can't even begin to imagine."

Olivia could feel their options slipping away quickly. Whoever the Gamemaster was, they seemed to have thought of every possibility. It seemed that there was no chance of them getting out of playing whatever sick game they had in mind. Olivia swallowed.

"Please don't do anything rash. We're willing to cooperate with you. No one needs to get hurt…"

The Gamemaster laughed. "Oh, I don't know about that. But at least for now, you're right. I'd like to have some fun before the blood starts spilling. And that means getting you here. I'll cut you a very, very generous deal. If you come to the island and play my games with the other contestants… you can walk away from the games with as many survivors as you're able to save. Twelve of you will fight for your lives on this island… some will live; some will die. I'll leave it up to you to spare as many as you can. You'll be the lifeline of some of these poor people. They wouldn't know how to save themselves if their lives depended on it… which they do."

The Gamemaster cackled once again. Olivia could feel the steam rising off of Brock. She was sure it was coming off of her just as hot. How could it not when the Gamemaster was threatening to kill so many people? Olivia had no idea about who the other "contestants" on the island were, but she knew that if they were just ordinary citizens, then these games were designed to hurt them—to kill them. The offer wasn't generous. It was blackmail.

Without Brock and Olivia, none of them would survive.

"Tell us the next step. We'll do whatever it takes," Olivia said firmly. She had no choice but to comply; she wasn't going to let people die on her watch if she could help it. She would always choose to help people, even if there was a cost to herself.

"Very good, Olivia. I knew you'd be fun to play with. I will send for someone to transport you from Washington to our top-secret location. You will *not* allow the authorities to track your location or to follow you. And if I find out you've broken the rules… what's going to happen?"

Olivia pursed her lips. "You'll kill everyone."

"Very good. You catch on quick. You will have to survive seven days on the island. After that, you'll all be free to go… if you make it that far. You will be tested in every way possible—physically, mentally, socially… it will push you to your limits."

"I'm already at my limits," Brock growled. "If I ever get ahold of you…"

"Careful, Brock. It's not going to win you any supporters if you threaten the host," the Gamemaster chuckled.

"I'll do what you ask. I'll play your stupid game. But just answer me one thing," Brock said. "Why? Why are you doing this? Threatening innocent lives… you have no idea what Yara has been through."

"Don't I?" The Gamemaster asked, cocking their head to the side. "I know a lot more than you think, Brock. I know the strengths and weaknesses of every single person I brought to this island… I picked the contestants myself, whether they realized it or not. I know yours too. I know that you defeated ANH, and I know you're capable of incredible things. Though it goes without saying that your weakness is sitting right next to you…"

Olivia felt her cheeks heat up. How did this person know so much about them all? Was it someone they had faced before? Something was very off about the whole thing. It didn't seem real. But it was, and they weren't being given many options. If they couldn't pull it together, blood would be spilled.

The Gamemaster let out a bloodcurdling cackle. "Oh, this will be a delight! It's not every day you get to enlist two FBI agents to your gameshow. I think you'll both have some surprises in store for me too." Olivia could tell they were smiling behind their golden mask.

"Now, you have twenty-four hours before your transport arrives at the airport… I expect that you'll arrive alone and that you won't do anything stupid, like enlist your FBI friends. One of my best pilots will personally take you to the island, and then we can get on with things. But if you refuse… you know what will happen. So don't be late! And happy gaming!"

Before Olivia or Brock could say another word, the call ended. Olivia had never seen Brock look so furious. He curled his hands into fists.

"What the hell are we going to do now? How are we going to get around this?"

Olivia shook her head. "We're not. We're playing the Gamemaster's game now."

CHAPTER THREE

"**J**ONATHAN ISN'T GOING TO LIKE THIS," OLIVIA said to Brock as they got into his car.

Brock scoffed. "And we do?"

"He's not going to settle for us going anywhere. He hates giving in to the demands of tyrants; we both know that."

"This is different. Civilian lives are at stake."

"Maybe, but he'll see it as a trap," Olivia reasoned. "He won't want to send us in there unarmed when there are too many unpredictable variables. He'll be thinking logically about how many lives he'll save if he doesn't send us out there. He'll expect everyone on the island to die."

"They definitely will if we don't go."

"That's not the point. You didn't see how much he was against the idea of sending out a team to find you."

"Oh, well that's charming," Brock mused.

"You know how he is. He's weighing it in terms of how many people we can save. He'll see our going out there as a suicide mission. And he might be right. What do we know about the Gamemaster and their plans? How do we know it's even possible to get out of there alive?"

"We don't. But that's not going to change your mind about going, is it?" Brock asked.

Olivia sighed. He was right, of course. She had made her mind up already. If there was a possibility that they could save lives, then they had to go. The Gamemaster had made their rules clear: the only chance of the contestants surviving was if they agreed to go along with the terms. That left them with no other choice, as far as Olivia was concerned.

And Olivia knew Brock felt the same, deep down. He wasn't going to allow Yara to die alone on an island because they refused the call. He'd do whatever it took to save his friend because that was how he lived his life. For better or worse, Olivia knew they were both going to be on a plane in twenty-four hours, headed into the unknown.

They just had to face their family and friends first.

Jonathan was their first port of call. They were driving up to DC. Neither of them had bothered to pack a bag, certain that they wouldn't be allowed to take anything with them on their possible one-way trip. Olivia's passport and gun were tucked into her pocket, but she didn't imagine she'd be allowed to keep her weapon. It just gave her the illusion of safety for now, and it would continue to until she was aboard the Gamemaster's plane.

"No matter how he tries to dissuade us, we have to make sure he doesn't stop us," Brock murmured, his grip strong on the steering wheel. "We don't have time to be fighting him on this one."

"I know."

"And Olivia?"

"Yeah?"

"If we make it out of this alive, we need to talk," Brock said. Olivia's heart skipped a beat.

"Talk?"

"Yes. Not about you and me… but about us working together," Brock said. Olivia frowned, staring at Brock to see if he was serious. She couldn't read his stoic expression.

"I don't understand what you mean."

"We'll talk later," Brock insisted. They'd arrived at their destination. Neither of them had called ahead to let Jonathan know they were coming, but Olivia was certain he'd still be in his office, even at such a late hour. He often stayed late, slaving his life away behind a desk to keep the FBI operational. For once, that was going to work in their favor.

Olivia desperately wanted to push Brock on the subject of their career together, but she knew it wasn't the right time. She had to be ready to talk to Jonathan, and that was going to take all the energy she had left in her. But it worried her that Brock had his doubts. She couldn't imagine a world where they didn't work together anymore, and the fact that he was considering it made her stomach churn with nerves.

They found Jonathan hunched over his computer in his office. It wasn't often Olivia saw him so late in the day since she'd usually gone home already, but she had to admit he looked a little ragged. There were cups of coffee strewn all over his desk, and his eyes were ringed with dark circles. It didn't seem like a great time to tell him what was going on, but there was no going back now. Time wasn't on their side.

He looked surprised when they entered his office uninvited, like he wasn't used to seeing another soul so late at night. Perhaps he didn't get many visitors at close to midnight.

"Tanner, Knight… what are you doing here?" Jonathan asked, straightening his back with what looked to be some difficulty. Olivia and Brock exchanged a glance. Neither of them wanted to be the one to talk first. Brock stepped forward, gripping the seat opposite Jonathan's.

"We're in a conundrum," Brock told him. "We received a call a couple of hours ago from Yara Montague. She was flying out of

LA on her way to a retreat… but when she called, the plane was going down. Apparently, the plane went way off course before it started plummeting toward the ocean. And then we received another call from her cell… but it was someone else. Someone called the Gamemaster."

Jonathan sat forward, his brow furrowed. "The Gamemaster, huh? I've heard of them. They've been causing some major issues in recent years. They're constantly pushing the boundaries of the law, but we haven't been able to find the person responsible. Are you saying that the Gamemaster has taken your friend?"

Olivia swallowed. "It's worse than that, sir. They have issued a direct invitation to Brock and me; we are supposed to be participating."

His eyes flared. "What?"

"It's a death match of sorts. We weren't given many details, but the Gamemaster has summoned us to an island to survive trials with the survivors of the apparent plane crash. We're supposed to be tested, pushed to our limits. And if we bring any backup or other agents, everyone else will be killed."

"Yara's there. We have to go," Brock insisted. Jonathan shook his head immediately.

"Absolutely not."

"If we don't go, everyone else will be killed," Olivia continued. "We're not being given a choice."

"I said no. You need my permission to go, and I'm not giving it. You're two of my best agents. I can't have another situation like what happened with ANH."

Olivia's shoulders sagged. She wouldn't forget what happened on the last remote island the FBI visited in a hurry. So many agents had lost their lives there. Henry Caine, her contact with MI5, had almost been killed and had lost his legs. It was something she thought about all the time, and she carried the guilt with her. But what choice did they have this time? The Gamemaster had made it personal, and there was no going back from that.

"If the Gamemaster wants us dead, I can guarantee they won't stop just because we don't go to the island," Brock pointed. "They will hunt us down—maybe even make a sport of it, since they love games so much. You know deep down that this isn't a choice we are being given. We have to go. People will die if we don't."

"People will die if you *do*."

"Maybe, but fewer," Olivia pressed. "The Gamemaster promised us that there would be ways for us all to survive… but only if Brock and I go there."

Olivia hoped he would see that they didn't have a choice. If he said no, it would mean condemning Yara and the others on the island to death. She didn't think she could handle that on her conscience.

"Why is it always you two getting into trouble?" Jonathan murmured, his index finger and thumb pinching the bridge of his nose as if to stave off an impending migraine. "You do realize that you're putting me in an impossible situation? How can you expect me to just sign off on this?"

"You have to let us go, sir," Brock pleaded. "Not just for Yara… but for the others on that island. I refuse to stay here and let them die. Our job is to protect innocent people. And that's what we'll go out there to do. And you know you can't help us. No reinforcements, no trying to track our location… we have to go alone."

"The Gamemaster made the rules clear. One wrong step and everyone dies," Olivia whispered. "We won't do anything to risk the Gamemaster turning on us."

"I'm sorry. I can't allow this," Jonathan insisted. "There's no—"

He was interrupted by the sound of Olivia slamming her badge on the desk. She reached into her pocket and pulled out her gun, too, placing it down a little more gently.

"We have to do this, sir," she said. "I'll never be able to live with myself if we don't. Neither will Brock. And you know that."

Brock had been looking at her, stunned, when he gave an imperceptible nod and put his own badge on the desk as well. "We can't just leave her to die. I don't care if I'm throwing my career away."

Olivia's heart soared. She had taken a leap of faith, and it would pay off. Who knew what the future would hold—if there even was a future for them? But no matter what happened on the island, whether they lived or died, they would do it together. There was no doubt at all that they were in trouble. But if there was one thing Olivia knew about herself and Brock, it was that they were survivors. They'd get through this, just as they got through everything else.

"Let's go, Brock."

Olivia threaded her fingers into Brock's and turned to leave, but Jonathan stopped them. "Wait."

She turned back. Jonathan looked so tired in that moment that it made Olivia's heart sink. They'd all seen way more than they should in a lifetime. How much torture could they all endure before they snapped? It came with the territory of the job, and yet sometimes it felt like it was too much to handle.

He held up the badges that they'd unceremoniously slammed on the desk and shook them. "Don't forget these."

Olivia was touched. "Sir?"

He sighed and ushered them back in. "I'll figure out the paperwork. But you have to promise something."

"What's that?" Brock asked. Jonathan's chest heaved.

"That you make this all worth it. That you make sure you get out alive. That's an order."

Brock offered Jonathan a grave smile. "Yes, sir."

CHAPTER FOUR

It was twelve hours before it was time for Olivia and Brock to head to the airport. They had tried to get some shut-eye in a hotel, but Olivia was sure that Brock slept as little as she did. She tossed and turned for hours, and when a fitful sleep took her, she kept jolting awake with anxiety.

Just like the good old days, she thought. It had been a while since insomnia called her name, but now it was just like an old friend to her. As she lay awake, she thought of what the days ahead would hold for her, whether she could handle it, whether she'd make it through. She tortured herself until daylight arrived and then prepared herself for the final hours of normality she had left.

Now, it was nearing noon, and Olivia knew she had to face calling her parents. She couldn't bear the thought of leaving without telling them where she was going. She had enough trauma from her mother's disappearance to ever just go without a word. She couldn't bear the idea of leaving them in the dark and scaring them the way she'd been scared.

As she called her mother, she wondered if this would be the last time they'd ever speak. Olivia had gone up against the odds plenty of times before, but she was sure that her luck would run out at some point, and then what could she do? Her whole life, she felt like she was being chased by something dark and ominous. Maybe this was the time it would truly catch up to her.

It took Jean a while to respond to the call, and when she did, it was clear she was in the middle of something. She had her phone propped up against the wall, and there was hissing sound like something was frying in the background. The normality of her cooking in the background made Olivia tear up a little.

"Olivia, darling, this isn't the best time. My book club is coming over, and I'm supposed to have made them all breakfast," Jean told her. Olivia's heart squeezed. It wasn't often she saw her mom so calm, so domestic. She didn't want to ruin the moment for her by saying what she needed to say. But she had to.

"Mom… this is kind of important. I don't want to interrupt, but… I need to talk to you."

Jean frowned and looked at the camera. "What's wrong, honey? Are you and Brock doing okay?"

"We're… we're fine, Mom. It's kind of more important than that. Brock and I… we have to go away for work."

Jean looked relieved for a moment. "Oh, I see. How long will you be gone for? Going anywhere exciting?"

Olivia scrambled for words. How was she ever going to explain this to her without her freaking out? Olivia understood the weight of being the only surviving daughter. Her family had been through so much already. And now she was shipping off to some deserted island where she might well lose her life.

"The thing is… well, it's going to be dangerous. Brock and I… we were called upon to save an island full of people. We… we're going to be live streamed as we… fight for our lives."

Jean's face dropped once again. "What on earth are you talking about?"

"There's this… this public figure… the Gamemaster. They've been doing crazy stunts for years while racking up millions of viewers. And now… they're hosting some kind of crazy games. Deadly games. Brock's friend has been dragged into it against her will. And now we've been summoned to play… or else everyone on the island will die."

Jean shook her head. "This… this is madness. The FBI needs to do something about it!"

"It's too risky, Mom. If we don't play by the rules, then more people are going to get hurt…"

"And what about my daughter? What about you, Olivia? You're just expected to go there and sacrifice yourself? Tell me you're not considering it!"

"You know I am, Mom. And I know if the tables were turned, you'd already be on a plane by now. Like you did before."

That shut her up. Olivia hated to pull that card, but it was the only thing she could do.

"Don't be like this, please, Mom. You know I wouldn't have it any other way. I don't have a choice, but even if I did, I'd go. There are innocent lives at stake. I won't be the reason that those people die. Not if there's even a slight chance that I can save them."

Jean pressed her palm to her chest, as if trying to control the beating of her own heart. She shook her head, closing her eyes. "I… I don't believe this. This shouldn't be happening. Not to you. Not after… not after everything we've already endured. I swear the world just tests us over and over again."

"I know. I'm sorry. I wish there was another way. But you understand why I have to go, don't you?"

Jean's expression softened. "I… yes. Yes, I do. Of course, I get it. My brave, brave daughter… you have so much power in you. I don't think you even realize it sometimes."

Olivia swallowed down the lump in her throat. It was in the rare moments when Jean let her guard down that she said such emotional things. Olivia knew that in Jean's head, she was preparing to say goodbye, not knowing whether they'd ever speak again. And suddenly, Olivia felt more determined than ever that she would make it home, no matter the cost. She had so much to live for, so much left unsaid. She couldn't leave it all behind. Not without fighting for what she was owed. She and her family had so much unfinished business that she wasn't prepared to leave behind.

"It's going to be okay, Mom," Olivia whispered. "I know you're scared… but you have to trust in me. Trust in my abilities."

Jean took a deep breath and smiled sadly at her daughter. "That's one thing I can trust in. But I can't trust whoever put you in this position to play fair. You're being used for entertainment. There's no chance that this person is willing to let you off lightly. You have to be stronger, smarter, craftier. Play them at their own game. Play dirty if you have to."

Olivia laughed. "You don't need to tell me twice. I'll do anything to get home. To get *everyone* home."

"I know. Just… just come back to me. Please." Jean's voice cracked a little. "I don't want to lose you. My baby girl."

"You won't," Olivia said firmly. "I'm ready for anything they throw at me. And this time, I'll have Brock by my side. You don't need to worry."

"As if I'm not going to worry. Besides, you know I love Brock, but you're more competent than he'll ever be."

Olivia laughed, wiping a tear from her eye, but Jean's face remained sullen. She swallowed.

"How long until you leave?"

Olivia swallowed. "I have to be at the airport at nine. A private jet is being sent to pick us up… and we have to go alone. That was part of the rules. No protection, no backup."

Jean closed her eyes, shaking her head. "Sometimes, I think the world has thrown everything it can at us. But I guess it still has more in store."

"That's all right," Olivia murmured. "I've got plenty more in store too. The Gamemaster won't know what hit them."

Jean smiled. "That's my girl."

CHAPTER FIVE

OLIVIA AND BROCK WERE SILENT IN THE CAR ON THE way to the airport. Jonathan had organized for a trusted driver to take them there, but after that, they would be on their own, just as the Gamemaster had demanded. The airport had been made aware of the issue and had cleared a runway to allow Olivia and Brock to board. They would be escorted as far as the plane door and then they would be on their own. It was getting more serious by the second; they were all under the Gamemaster's thumb now.

"Do you think the Gamemaster is watching?" Olivia whispered to Brock on their approach. She was sure that the Gamemaster would have some way to examine their arrival and make sure they were following the rules. He set his jaw.

"Oh, you can bet on it. And not just the Gamemaster. The whole world. Word will be spreading as we speak. Everyone will be tuning in to see if we live or die. It's sick."

Olivia reached for his hand across the backseat. "Don't give in to your anger. I'm furious too. But we have to keep our wits about us. We have to stay levelheaded and calm. We don't want to make any mistakes."

"How am I supposed to be calm? The Gamemaster kidnapped one of my dearest friends, threatened innocent civilians, gave us an impossible choice… and now they're throwing you into the fire too. That's a surefire way to get on my bad side," Brock said through gritted teeth. Olivia felt her expression soften.

"Hey. It's going to be okay. I can handle myself."

"I know you can, in normal circumstances. But this is different. Do you really think the Gamemaster is going to allow us to get out alive? *Both* of us? Where's the fun in that? He's looking for drama, for emotion, for a way to keep the world watching. He's going to put his thumb on the scales. He won't let both of us survive. It wouldn't fit his little game."

"Brock, you're spiraling."

"Of course, I'm spiraling! Don't you understand what we're walking into? One of us—at the most—might make it home, but that's it," he snapped tersely. "The Gamemaster is going to see potential in the fact that we're together and try to kill one of us for the entertainment value. The fact that you don't see that makes me even more scared for us. One of us will die this week. I don't want to walk out of this without you."

Olivia felt her mouth drop open. How could Brock talk like that? After everything he'd survived, he was talking about giving up his life if he didn't have her? He was willing to just let it happen if it meant she'd survive?

"Brock, please…"

"This is what I wanted to talk to you about, Olivia. I can't do this anymore. Working with you is too hard. It feels like the world is using our relationship against us. Every step we take together, our enemies find ways to hurt us—to use the other as a weapon."

"That doesn't matter though," she pushed back. "We've been through so much together. We've survived everything they've thrown at us. We've done it before, and we can do it again. Whatever it takes."

"Until our luck runs out," he said. Olivia's heart sank. She'd been thinking the same things herself, and Brock knew it. How long did they really have until their luck ran out? How many more times could they leap into the wild unknown and overcome impossible odds before the consequences finally caught up with them?

How many more times could they escape certain death unscathed?

Olivia didn't know. She didn't want to know. For that matter, she didn't care. All she cared about was that wherever Brock was going, she would go too—even if that meant putting herself in danger.

"What are you saying, Brock? You don't want to be together anymore?" Olivia said slowly. She couldn't believe he was doing this right before one of the scariest missions of their lives. Brock sighed, running his hand through his hair.

"I'm not saying that at all, Olivia. I'm saying that maybe… maybe we'd be better off with different partners."

"You know that's not true," Olivia replied. "You couldn't investigate your way out of a paper bag without me."

The joke lingered in the air and quickly went stale. Neither of them laughed. Both were just too wound up to even feel like they'd be able to let a single moment of levity in.

"I know. But none of that is even going to matter if we don't get out of here alive. And I'm starting to think that none of this was designed to let us escape."

Olivia's chest tightened. This was the last thing she wanted to hear. Working with Brock had changed her life. It had *become* her life. She loved working with him just as much as she loved their downtime together. For her, part of building their life together was working cases side by side, learning from one another, having each other's backs. Brock had expressed doubts before, and she knew that he was under more pressure than ever, but she couldn't face the thought of turning her back on their way of life together. It meant way too much to her.

But there were more pressing matters. They'd made it to the airport runway. Brock seemed to sense that he'd brought up the topic at a terrible time. He glanced her way with guilt in his eyes, and then squeezed her hand.

"We can't think about that now. It's an issue for later. If we make it that far," he said. "But just know that no matter what, I'm getting you out of this alive. You and Yara. That's my goal. Even if it kills me."

"You can't say things like that."

"I can. Ever since we've been together, I've been putting your life in danger. You've always been a target because of me."

"Not because of you," she snapped. "Plenty of people were chasing me down before you ever showed up in my life. What's the matter with you?"

"ANH tried to kill you because of me."

"You forget that ANH was after me too. After my sister. It's not all about you, Brock. I'm in this just the same as you. I have demons of my own chasing me. Don't forget that." She said it evenly, level; not mad at Brock but frustrated they had to have these conversations at such a tense moment.

"Not if it gets you in trouble. I'm done with that. The Gamemaster wanted me because of Yara, because of my connection to ANH—"

"If the Gamemaster only wanted you, then I wouldn't be coming with you. But they chose us both."

"I refuse to believe that he needed us both. He chose you to hurt me. He chose Yara to hurt me. This is personal, and you know it."

"I'm your girlfriend, Brock. Wherever you're concerned, of course, it's personal. Personal to me too. I would never have allowed you to go to the island alone if that was an option. I would've been by your side. I'll *always* be by your side."

Brock stared at Olivia for a long moment, trying to figure her out. She stared him down, too, refusing to back down. He had to understand that he mattered to her just as much as she mattered to him. How could she ever let him face such danger alone? Didn't he understand that whatever they did, they did it together? It wasn't a matter of pride or trying to be a hero. It was just a simple fact—they always had one another's back. She would've felt that way about it long before they were ever a couple.

She would never leave him to face the world alone.

"My decision is final. I'm getting reassigned to a new partner if we make it back. You can fight me on it as much as you like, should it come to that. But you should respect how I feel about it. I would do the same for you if the tables were turned," Brock said.

Then he got out of the car, and Olivia felt frustration rising inside her. This was all a symptom of the games the Gamemaster had laid out for them, and she knew it; but it didn't stop the fury and pain inside her chest from taking hold. It hurt her how eager Brock seemed to turn his back on everything they'd built, everything they'd risked, at the very first hurdle.

Brock was right, they needed to get out alive before they could discuss their future. And yet still, the thought of parting ways with Brock in any capacity was a thought she didn't want to entertain. He might feel differently about it now, but a few days earlier, he never would've said those things. She had time to change his mind, and she vowed that she would.

Olivia cursed under her breath as she, too, got out of the car. The crisp wind whipped at her face as she stared down the private plane that would take them to the island. She clenched her fists.

If there was going to be a winner, it was going to be her. She'd make sure of it.

CHAPTER SIX

THE PLANE WAS GIVING OLIVIA CLAUSTROPHOBIA. AS SHE and Brock sat tight on the white, leather seats, she couldn't relax. Not even in the height of luxury. She'd never been on a private jet before, but even with the bottle of champagne in a cooling bucket and the swanky furniture, Olivia saw past it all to the horrors they were about to endure. The plane was likely an illusion to make them relax. She couldn't allow herself to forget how sinister their situation was.

And it didn't help that Brock had barely said a word to her since they boarded the plane. She knew he was anxious, and she knew on some level they were likely being watched, but he had closed himself off entirely. Though his hand remained on her knee, he didn't look at her, opting instead to stare out the window at the waters below. Olivia had to wonder where they were being taken. They'd been on the plane for a few hours now. For a while, she had busied herself with picturing a world map, trying to imagine where they might be flying to, but she soon gave up. She almost didn't want to know.

All that mattered was them getting there safely. Then, they'd rescue Yara and the other survivors. Whatever would be thrown at them, they could handle it. Unlike Brock, Olivia truly believed that they were capable of getting out of there alive. A game with no winner would look bad on the Gamemaster. They would be pushed to their limits, but they'd come through the other end. She was sure of it. Because how many trials had they faced in their lifetime? What could possibly be worse than they'd already endured?

The Gamemaster had told them they'd be tested physically, mentally and socially, issues they easily got around every single day in their line of work. They were at their peak physically, they had plenty of experience socially, and they were two mentally strong individuals. What could go wrong?

Well, a lot could go wrong. She didn't want to get overconfident. Who knew what horrific designs awaited them on the island, what monstrous traps lay in wait to snare them? But Olivia was strong. And though he doubted himself, Brock was too. They couldn't go into this with the mindset that only one of them would survive. They had to work together, to be in lockstep every step of the way. It was their only chance.

Olivia stood up and stretched her legs, pacing around the small space. She didn't really want to look anxious for the cameras, but she needed something to do with herself. It was driving her wild to sit still. Brock shot her a warning glance, but she ignored it. If he wasn't going to talk to her, then she didn't have to live by his rules, for sure.

There was a crackle of static above Olivia's head, and she looked up expectantly, her heart skipping a beat. Brock was immediately on his feet, placing a comforting hand on her arm. They both waited, holding their breath. Olivia had no doubt in her mind that they were about to hear from the Gamemaster. But why so soon? They couldn't be at their destination yet…

"Good evening, my lovely contestants," the Gamemaster's distorted voice sounded out. "Welcome to the festivities. Your first challenge is about to begin."

"What?" Brock snapped. "We're not at the island yet. This wasn't part of the deal."

Olivia nudged his arm as subtly as she could. The last thing they needed was to let the Gamemaster get under their skin. They should've known better—the fancy plane and the leisurely ride was too good to be true. They would be tested now because it would entertain the Gamemaster's followers. That was how it worked.

"You are now live to over five million streamers worldwide. You've made me *very* popular all of a sudden. So, I thank you for that."

"Anytime," Brock huffed sarcastically. Olivia couldn't help but crack a slight smile. Even with his back against the wall, even with the world falling apart around them, Brock never lost his wit.

It just might be the thing to save them both.

"Oh, believe me, Mr. Tanner, you will find yourself suited quite well for the spotlight. Comments are rolling in from around the world about how much viewers look forward to seeing you. Some wish to see you win. And some… wish to see you suffer."

The way he said it made Olivia's skin crawl.

"And don't think you're off the hook either, Ms. Knight. I've been listening, you know. I assure you, you are not here merely as an accessory to Brock. I have my own designs for you. Designs that will push you past every shred of self-control you always had. What kind of feminist would I be otherwise?"

Olivia blinked. "You—huh—what?"

The Gamemaster shrieked in vile, chilling laughter. "Oh, this will be such fun! Now, with no further ado, the games simply must begin. I thought I would go easy on you to begin with."

Brock scoffed, but had the sense not to say anything further. Olivia waited for more to come. She was anxious, but in control. She wouldn't allow her feelings to get in the way of their survival.

"Consider this plane to now be an escape room," the Gamemaster said with a low chuckle. "I have secured two parachutes and two life vests somewhere on this plane. You will have sixty minutes to find them and put them on in preparation to exit the plane. After that… well, let's just say that if you're still on the plane in sixty minutes, you won't survive much longer. I have set the plane to self-destruct on my command…"

Olivia and Brock traded a panicked look, but remained silent.

"Fun, right? So don't waste any time! And give us a show, will you? If you're boring to watch… I may just blow up the plane anyway. Joking! Or… am I?"

Olivia gritted her teeth. The Gamemaster had all the power in their hands. They could do whatever they wanted whenever they wanted, no matter whether Olivia and Brock did as they were told or not. But not following the rules would certainly get them killed. They had to at least try to appease their cruel puppet master, even though it went against every single one of Olivia's instincts. But that meant throwing themselves into the task. There was no more time to waste being upset at the unfairness of the situation.

"Your time will start in exactly one minute. Or has it already started? Did it start as soon as you heard my voice? Who knows… maybe you'd better start searching."

Olivia immediately whipped her head around to survey the plane. She didn't want to look desperate, but sixty minutes wasn't a long time. She and Brock had been to several escape rooms in the past. Some they had solved easily… others they hadn't solved at all. Olivia was betting this would be a lot more complicated than the average escape room. The Gamemaster wanted to see them both squirm.

Or get blown to smithereens.

"All right, we can do this," Olivia said, trying to convince herself more than anything. "We're going to do this, all right? What do we have to work with?"

She began to explore the room. She checked under the seats they were sitting on. She examined the champagne bucket and the ice, thinking they might be well placed props, but she didn't see anything out of the ordinary. Brock had finally made a move and was checking the emergency exits. Olivia didn't relish the thought that in less than an hour, they'd be forced to jump out of there. It had been a long time since she had jumped from such a height, and only for the purpose of training. But their hands were being forced. None of the situation was going to be ideal, and they'd just have to make do.

"Nothing under the seats," Brock reported.

"Nothing over here either." She tried the door to the pilot's room, but it was locked. She knocked hard and shouted for the pilot, but there was no response. Not that she expected one. With their luck, the pilot was already dead, and the plane was just on autopilot. Or maybe there had never been a pilot to begin with. They didn't see one before taking off, so she truly had no idea.

The more Olivia searched, the more she felt like they were being trolled. There were several cabinets, but all of them were locked with no signs of keys or combinations to unlock them. Olivia knew there had to be answers somewhere, but wherever they were, they weren't sticking out to her.

And that's when her eyes fell on the clock. She'd spotted it when they arrived on the plane, but hadn't looked at it since. The time stood at the same as when they took off. She took a closer look to check where the hands were sitting. The time was frozen on thirteen minutes past four.

"I think this has to mean something," Olivia told Brock, pointing at the clock. "I think it could be a combination of some sort. Some variation of the numbers thirteen and zero four. There are a bunch of padlocks in here… four numbers would likely open at least one of them."

"It's worth a shot," Brock said. He looked tired, and Olivia understood. These games were ridiculous and scary, and she didn't want to play with so much at stake. She didn't imagine she'd ever enjoy games again. And they certainly wouldn't be going back to an escape room when all this was over. But if they had the answer in front of them, they had to put it to use. There was no time to mope around.

"Let's try it over here," Olivia said, hurrying over to one of the cupboards. It looked large enough to hold the items they were looking for. Her hands felt a little unsteady as she put in as many variations of the numbers as she could think of. 1304. 0413. 3140. 4031. She kept going, but she couldn't feel the click of the padlock. She shook her head.

"We should try another one."

Olivia searched the room and found a white footlocker near the cockpit. She hadn't been able to open it before, but it looked like the perfect place to find something of use to them. She tried the combinations again, and the first four she tried didn't work. But when she tried 3410, the padlock gave way with a satisfying click. Excitement squeezed at her chest, but when she flung the box open, she found it to be empty. She hung her head and groaned in frustration.

"Okay, not this then."

"Maybe the combination is a red herring. We should look for something else," Brock said. Olivia scowled.

"You can look. I'll keep trying the combinations. It feels significant."

Brock started knocking on the walls and ceiling without another word, and Olivia continued searching alone. She found padlocks in the strangest of places, like on the underside of one of the seats and on the back of the overhead TV, but she couldn't see how they'd be significant. She walked down back to the set of cupboards in the bar area and set her sight on a cupboard above her head. Determined, she reached out and put in the original number. 0413.

It clicked open.

Olivia felt relief tug at her heart. She must have wasted fifteen minutes already. As she tugged open the cupboard, she expected to find something of use.

And that was when the first scorpion spilled out from overhead.

Olivia shrieked.

CHAPTER SEVEN

IT WAS EMBARRASSING TO SCREAM LIKE A LITTLE GIRL WHEN confronted with an insect, but at the same time, giant scorpions were raining onto her face, so it felt justified. She stumbled away from the overhead locker as scorpions continued to spill out, their stingers primed to kill; she swatted away at her face and chest until most of them had fallen onto the floor. Her heart was in her throat. What the hell was going on?

"Get back!" Brock cried out, rushing forward with an empty box. Olivia looked around for something she could use as a weapon, as a way to get the scorpions away, at least. She saw a broom leaning against a cupboard they'd just looked through and grabbed it, pushing scorpions away from her with panic rising in her chest. One of them somehow made the leap from the broom handle to her wrist, but one well-placed smack from her other hand forced it to drop to the ground. She stomped around a little more, squishing the bugs under her feet, but for every one she killed, three more swarmed in. She didn't know what she had expected from their experience on the plane to the island, but it certainly wasn't this.

There seemed to be hundreds of the black creatures swarming the plane. Olivia had no idea how they were supposed to deal with them without getting themselves seriously hurt. Brock tossed the box on top of a bunch of the creatures, sealing them beneath it, but there were still many, many more on the prowl. Olivia methodically shoved them away from them with the handle of her broom, but as soon as she'd pushed them away, it felt like the others were right at her ankles.

"Get them to the other side of the plane. I'll try to block them off," Brock said, leaping his way through the scorpions as they turned their attention on him. He managed to get through the group of them unscathed, but Olivia knew that the angry creatures would have no qualms with killing them both if they got the opportunity. Olivia felt one scuttle across her boot and instinctively smashed the broom against it, leaving it motionless beside her. She had never had much fear of scorpions before, but then again, she'd never expected to be trapped in a plane with hundreds of them.

On the opposite side of the plane, Brock was being swarmed by the scorpions, but he was busy building himself a pen out of any furniture he could grab, trapping the scorpions away from him. Olivia pushed the scorpions in the same direction, heading for the corner, so that Brock could trap them in. She didn't have time to think about how their stingers were much too close for comfort and they were riled up from being stuck in the cupboard. She just kept pushing on, hoping that she wouldn't get stung in the process.

They were beginning to pile up in the corner of the plane, a terrifying mound of deadly writhing creatures. Brock had grabbed one of the modern chairs from the plane to block one side of the mound while Olivia held the rest back with the broomstick.

"Hurry!" Olivia cried. The scorpions were beginning to slide down again, and she was sure they'd soon figure out how to get out of their poorly constructed enclosure. Brock returned with a pile of boxes, shoving them against the other side of the pile. It was no perfect solution, but they didn't have time for perfection. They still had to figure out the escape room, and they couldn't do that if scorpions were attacking them from every angle. Brock found a tablecloth stored in a cupboard and tossed it over the pile. Olivia didn't know if it would be enough to stop the scorpions from escaping, but they just had to hope it was.

"Jeez," Brock said, running a hand through his hair. "That was close."

"We're not done," Olivia said, shaking her head. "We still don't know how to get out of here."

"There's one more padlock," Brock said a little breathlessly, nodding to a strange chest in the opposite corner of the room. Olivia had assumed it was a storage bin for something, but she hadn't been sure what. "We will have to try it."

"What if there's something in there? Something dangerous again?"

"Do we have any choice? If we don't look, the plane is going down anyway," Brock reminded her. "We're out of time and out of luck."

"All right. We'll try the combinations."

Brock moved to the box and bent down, starting to input the numbers from the codes they'd come up with. Olivia kept an eye on the poorly constructed scorpion trap on the other end of the plane. If even one got out, she knew she would be back in full-on panic mode. She'd be seeing those things in her nightmares, for sure.

"Damn it," Brock muttered as his fingers fumbled with the padlock. "I can't think of any more combinations…"

"Try the original one," Olivia prompted him. Brock nodded decisively and tried it. He looked relieved, then super alert when the padlock fell away and the box was able to be opened. He cautiously flipped the lid and checked what was inside, both of them holding their breaths.

But there was no sign of any life jackets or parachutes. Inside the box was an old, gnarled key that looked like it wouldn't function in any ordinary lock. Olivia closed her eyes momentarily. The Gamemaster was taking them for a ride now. That much was obvious to her. It didn't matter to their overlord whether they lived or died. Maybe there was no escape route at all. Maybe this whole thing had been a ruse, and they were just the warm-up for the main event. They'd be dead within the hour, and the civilians trapped on the island would be left to fight alone.

"This can't be it," Olivia murmured. Brock sighed, throwing his hands up.

"We've looked everywhere on this godforsaken plane. Where else could the supplies be?"

"We haven't looked everywhere," Olivia said quietly. She had her eye on the door to the cockpit. She roughly rattled it, but it was still locked. Then an idea came to her.

"Hand me that fire extinguisher."

Brock looked around and saw it in the back, near where the scorpions had come from. He stepped around the enclosure as delicately as he could, lifted it off its hook, and brought it back over. "You sure we won't need this?"

Olivia raised an eyebrow. "Brock, if this plane catches fire, putting it out is going to be the least of our problems."

"Good point."

Olivia took a breath to steel herself and lifted up the extinguisher. It was heavy, but it would do the job. She brought it down hard, once, twice against the door, the metal against metal clinking hollowly in the cabin.

Brock turned back. "Hope you're onto something. Our new friends aren't very happy…"

She risked a quick glance back to see that indeed, a line of scorpions had figured out how to climb the makeshift wall and were already on their way out. Brock was swatting them back down, trying to find some way to contain them, but there was only so much he could do.

Olivia returned her attention to the door and redoubled her efforts. She smacked the door again, harder, and this time the fire extinguisher left a dent in the metal of the door. Finally, some progress! She aimed squarely for the dent and smacked the door again and again and again until it widened and bent under the strain of the impact.

She glanced back to see how Brock was doing and was shocked. It wasn't good. Despite his best efforts, the scorpions had managed to climb all the way out of the pen. He was still able to squash them one by one as they emerged, but it wouldn't be long before the sheer numbers overwhelmed them.

"Brock!"

"Just get that door open, Olivia!"

She lifted the extinguisher high above her head and slammed it down with every ounce of strength she had; miraculously, something clicked. She reared back and kicked the door, and finally, the lock disengaged and popped open. She reached in and slid the door open easily now, but what she found dumbfounded her.

Olivia couldn't believe what she was seeing. Not only was the cockpit devoid of a pilot, but it was also stocked up with the supplies they needed: parachutes and life jackets were piled on the chair where the pilot would be. Olivia tried not to allow terror to take over as she looked out the front of the plane, clouds and endless blue sky greeting her vision. She knew they just needed to get kitted up and get out.

"Brock. The supplies were here the whole time. Hidden in plain sight," she said. Brock let out an angry grunt, abandoning the scorpions and barreling through to be at Olivia's side.

"I guess we should prepare to get out of here. We still have ten minutes," he said. Olivia nodded, grabbing for the supplies. Ten minutes sounded like plenty of time, but she still had to figure out the equipment she'd be using. It had been a long time since she'd had to use a parachute in her training days. But she knew she could do it.

She didn't have a choice.

Her heart was in her stomach as she geared up and headed for the plane door with Brock in tow. Thankfully, they'd been able to herd most of the scorpions away from them and kill the few stragglers that came their way. They only had two minutes now, and they had to time their jump just right. She pressed the emergency button that unlocked the door, pushing it open with great difficulty. Cold wind blasted her face in full force, and she shuddered, looking down at what was about to greet them.

But something wasn't right. There was no sign of land anywhere around. All that was below them was a blanket of blue water, beckoning them to their deaths. Olivia swallowed. If they jumped now, they would die. They'd be stranded in the middle of the ocean, and they'd freeze in no time. With nowhere in sight to swim to, their chances of survival were zero.

Olivia turned to Brock, her heart hammering inside her chest. He read her face intently, trying to figure out what she was thinking. She shook her head, feeling defeated.

"The Gamemaster lied to us. There's no way out," she shouted over the roaring wind. "If we jump, we die. If we stay here, we'll die too. The plane will go up in flames, and so will we."

Brock swallowed, his eyes closing for a brief moment. Olivia checked her watch. They had one minute left. She reached for Brock's hand, trying not to let her emotions get the better of her. She wasn't ready to let the world go. But she refused to cry.

That was what the Gamemaster wanted from her. And she would not give that monster the satisfaction.

"I'm not jumping," she told Brock. "I'm not dying slowly in the middle of the ocean. If we stay aboard, at least it'll be quick."

Brock nodded, swallowing again. He pulled her close and held her. They stood there as the wind roared in their ears, and Olivia felt weightless for a moment. It was over. There was nothing more to do.

"We had a good run, didn't we?" Brock murmured with a forced smile. Olivia smiled back.

"The best run," she whispered. She knew they only had seconds left to spare. She clung to him harder.

"I love you," she whispered, her voice swallowed by the wind. The countdown reached zero.

CHAPTER EIGHT

OLIVIA OPENED HER EYES SLOWLY, HER HEART IN HER throat. The countdown was over, and they were still standing, knees wobbling, at the exit. The sound of the Gamemaster's laughter echoed around the plane, and she blinked in disbelief.

What was going on?

And then it dawned on her. The Gamemaster wasn't going to blow them up. That would be a boring way for them to go out. It was too final. No, the Gamemaster might be willing to toy with them, but they weren't going to die so easily. Not when they could be tortured some more. She had to remind herself that they were soon to be contestants in the sickest game the world had ever seen. If they died before they made it to the island, that would be a pretty anticlimactic ending. The Gamemaster would never allow that. For some stupid reason, that made her feel safe.

"Very good," the Gamemaster chuckled. "You trusted your instincts, and you're still here because of it. Bravo! Aren't you having a lovely time? I know the audience is."

Olivia felt sick to her stomach. They'd survived, but what if they'd made the wrong decision? They'd be deep in the ocean by now, waves smashing against their bodies. The water would be ice cold, and they were way too far from land to survive for long. If they'd jumped, they'd be dead.

If they stayed, they'd likely be dead anyway.

Brock was trembling with rage beside her. She reached for his hand, and he held it tight, the only thing stopping him from blowing up with anger. They both understood without saying it aloud that they couldn't let their fear and frustration show, no matter how bad things got. They'd made it this far. The audience would at least be rooting for them now, wanting them to prove themselves further. Perhaps the Gamemaster would be more lenient with them from then on, since they were doing as they were told.

"I simply must say, I'm enjoying putting you through the motions," the Gamemaster purred. "You're crowd pleasers. That goes down well with me. Perhaps I'll cut you some slack from now on. Maybe we can do something a little less intense next time. Oh, it's all so exciting!"

Olivia hoped that would be the case, but she wasn't holding her breath. If this was all just a warm-up to the main events on the island, then what on earth would they face there? The scorpions alone were enough to make her wish she hadn't come. Add a deathly drop to it, and she could barely even keep her sanity straight. She almost wished she knew how to fly a plane so she could turn it back around and head home.

But she and Brock were better equipped for such high stakes than most. The others would need them in that respect. Olivia let her shoulders loosen a little. The immediate danger was gone. They just needed to hang on until the next obstacle was thrown their way.

Brock glanced at Olivia, squeezing her hand again. "Sit down and get some rest. We don't know how long we'll be on this damn flight for. I'll keep an eye out for trouble."

Olivia wanted to argue, but she knew Brock wouldn't stand for it. He was far from in the mood to discuss something in a civil manner. Olivia made for one of the leather chairs and curled her feet up on the seats, hugging them. She closed her eyes, and she could still see the horrible scorpions scurrying around her feet. It made her skin prickle, like they were running up and down her arms and legs. At least they'd contained that threat. She sat there, forcing her eyes to stay open, but eventually her tiredness got the better of her, and at some point, they must have closed.

She woke with a jolt as someone shook her shoulders. Her eyes snapped open, and she could see Brock's panicked face before her. The engine of the plane was making a horrible strange noise, a wretched sputtering like the engine was giving out. The smell of something burning filled the cabin and sent a jolt of dread into Olivia's heart. She looked around her, feeling the vibrations of the plane shaking her seat.

"I told you I could self-detonate the plane at any time," the Gamemaster's voice said from above their heads. "And that moment is now. Better strap on those parachutes. But hey, this time I'm giving you a fighting chance. If you jump at the right time, you might get close enough to the island to swim… Better hold your breath! I know the audience is!"

Olivia leapt to her feet and ran to the window. Sure enough, there was an island in sight, and they were flying right toward it. But how long did they have before the plane was going to blow? When did it make sense to jump? Olivia was a strong swimmer, but she knew the dangers the choppy waters would pose for them if they tried to swim. If they timed their jump wrong, they'd die. If they didn't jump before the plane blew, they'd die. But if they went too early, their chances of survival would minimize with every foot they were swept out into the water. Olivia looked at Brock in panic. She could see that he was just as distressed as she was.

"Choices, choices," the Gamemaster murmured. "Oh, don't you love this? I feel alive, don't you?"

Olivia ignored the omniscient voice. The Gamemaster would try their best to rile her, but she refused to listen. She rushed to strap the parachute to her back, the life vest still safely strapped to her chest. She hadn't used a parachute in years, and she hoped it would all come back to her now. She faced the open waters, her chest heaving as she gasped for air. It was a bad time to be having a panic attack.

"What if the Gamemaster is playing us again?" Brock hissed. Olivia shook her head.

"Odds are the same trick won't be played twice. And if that's the island, I'd rather take my chances, wouldn't you? This might be our only chance of survival."

Brock wavered for a moment before he gave her a grim nod. Olivia helped him strap on his parachute, then he hauled open the plane door once more, the wind hitting their faces. The plane was getting lower and lower, and the island was coming closer into view. Still, Olivia knew looks could be deceiving. It seemed close from high up in the air, but if they dropped now, they'd still be miles out. The thought of the cold water and the thrashing waves was enough to make her hold fast. She turned to Brock.

"We jump together. Okay?"

He offered a harrowing smile. "Of course."

Olivia turned her attention back to the water. All she could hear were the sounds of a failing engine. She was sure they'd need to jump soon. Her legs trembled as she stood on the precipice, half ready to go and half unable to unroot herself from the plane. She closed her eyes and took a steadying breath.

"I think we have to go!" she cried over the roaring engine. Brock nodded and took her hand in his.

"On three?"

"On three. One, two…"

They leaped together into the unknown. Olivia's stomach plummeted, and then moments later, the world exploded around her ears. The plane had gone up in flames and was nosediving toward the water. Olivia pulled her parachute and felt the moment it caught her, leveling her with Brock in the air. She wanted to scream, but her pride kept her mouth shut as she fell with grace.

But then something happened. Something sliced straight through her parachute. She felt the force of the falling plane debris piercing through the parachute. The impact was so hard that it shook her away from Brock and tore their grasp apart.

"No!"

Her eyes locked onto Brock's, panic seizing her heart.

And she began to fall.

CHAPTER NINE

OLIVIA FELT HER STOMACH DROP AS SHE FELL TOWARD the water. She knew what would happen to her when she hit the waves. She'd fallen from too high. The impact would kill her as her body slammed into the harsh waters. She looked up one last time and screamed Brock's name.

Only he was there beside her. Somehow, he'd tilted forward and reached down, and now his hand snagged the top of her life jacket, stopping her from falling. She gasped out in shock as she swung in midair, her body jolting from Brock's saving grip.

"You have to let go! I'm taking you down too fast!" Olivia cried hoarsely. Brock shook his head.

"Just get your parachute off your back! It's going to get all tangled!"

But there was no time. They were already too close to the water. Olivia braced herself for the cold, and it hit her hard, salt water filling her ears and stinging her closed eyes. She tried to keep her head above the water, gasping for fresh air, but the waves slammed straight back into her face. She could taste the water on her tongue. She tried not to swallow the water and to return her breathing to normal. If she was going to survive, she couldn't afford to panic. That also meant getting rid of the dead weight on her back.

Olivia allowed her lifejacket to do the work as she shrugged the parachute off her back. As soon as she was untangled, she raised her head as high as she could above the water, looking for Brock. It was hard to see much else other than blue all around her, the sky and sea seeming to blend into one.

"Brock!" Olivia cried out. She saw him appear as he bobbed above the waves, gasping for breath.

"Brock! Are you all right?"

"Never better," he croaked. He coughed as seawater filled his mouth. "We can't waste time. We have to swim for the shore. Probably not the best time to mention that swimming isn't my strong suit…"

"It's okay. I won't leave you. We can do this. But the faster we get there, the better."

Olivia began to swim toward Brock. The sun was starting to rise on the day, and she was already starting to worry about the heat of the sun. It would soon burn them and dehydrate them as they exerted themselves. *But one issue at a time*, she thought. She didn't want to dwell on what she couldn't control.

The sway of the current seemed to be against them, knocking into her side as she slowly crawled through the water to Brock. It would be hard going, but at least they had stamina. All those evenings jogging together in the woods might pay off now. It might be the only thing that would save them. Olivia chose to keep her eyes on the island as they swam in tandem, forcing themselves onward. She didn't want to know what lurked in the deep, dark blue below her. The ocean was so vast, so big in comparison to the two of them as they struggled on. It was full of creatures that knew those waters far better than she did. The thought terrified her, but she had to be strong. She could see that Brock was struggling, water lashing at his face with every stroke, but he carried onward with grim determination. The thought of him beside her kept her going. He had just saved her life. There was no chance she was giving up this opportunity to live.

And there was even less chance of her leaving Brock behind.

The island slowly came closer to them. Olivia had no real sense of time, but the sun seemed to be getting higher in the sky. She could feel the warmth of it against the chill of the waters. She only hoped that would stop them from freezing to death, even as the sun burned salt against her face.

But every stroke forward felt like it was followed by two strokes back. The waves were punishing and relentless, and they were both running out of steam. Olivia felt the moment that Brock's audible sigh was accompanied by him stopping. In the split second he stopped moving, the waves carried him further back. Panic seized her heart. She wasn't going to allow Brock to be swept away, but she wasn't sure she could drag him along with her. He was too heavy.

"You have to keep moving!" Olivia cried out. Her throat was sore. Brock shook his head, breathing hard.

"I won't make it."

"Of course, you will. I won't have it any other way. Keep moving, damn it!"

Brock finally began to slog forward again. Olivia waited for him, her eyes on the island. They were close now, it seemed. She knew they were probably farther away than she expected, that her excitement might be getting the better of her, but they were closer than they had been, and that was enough to encourage her. They could do it. They had to do it.

Her arms and legs ached, and as she began to move again, her muscles locked up with agonizing pain. But she pressed on because she was far from done. She wouldn't allow herself to die in the middle of the ocean where no one would ever find her. She'd make it to land if it was the last thing she did.

As the end of the journey neared, Olivia felt her vision blurring. Cold had set in deep in her bones. It felt like her body was giving up. She shuddered, pushing on. She couldn't see Brock beside her, but she hoped he was following her. She didn't have the energy to turn and see. If she did, she knew she might lose herself to the waves. She closed her eyes and prayed he was with her, that they'd both make it to the island in one piece.

And then she felt something beneath her. The waves around her were beginning to quiet, and her arms brushed something stringy. She opened her eyes. Her hands were tangled in seaweed, and she was only meters away from a sandy shore. Desperately, she clawed forward, feeling her hand dig into hot sand on the beach. She let out an exhausted laugh, falling forward with her cheek against the sand.

She'd made it.

She turned to see Brock trudging onto the beach beside her, his wet clothes weighing down his exhausted body. He fell to his knees just shy of her, lying down and trying to remember how to breathe again. Silent tears stained Olivia's face.

They'd done it. They'd beaten the first challenge.

Olivia wasn't sure how long they lay there, beaten down by the grueling swim. But when she opened her eyes again, it became clear that time had passed her by. The sun was high in the sky and burning her skin. She forced herself to sit up and saw Brock still lying where he was before. She stumbled over to him.

"Brock... we have to get to shade."

"Mmm," Brock grunted. He barely seemed conscious, but he managed to get to his feet like a zombie, and together they headed for the trees that lined the island. There, he sat right back down again while Olivia looked in her salvaged backpack for what supplies might be in there. There was a sealed bottle of water, and she took it out gratefully. She needed to rehydrate and wash the salt from her mouth. She drank and then passed it to Brock.

"We have to... we have to figure out what's next," she said. Her throat felt like someone had sliced through her windpipe. But she didn't care. They were alive, and for the moment, that was enough for her.

They were caught as if between two worlds. On one side was the endless expanse of ocean; on the other was densely wooded jungle. Olivia almost wanted to laugh. It was like she was in a movie.

"Where do you—"

Olivia was cut off by an anguished cry. Olivia and Brock exchanged a worried glance. Was that one of the contestants? It had to be. After all, who else would be on the island?

"Help!"

Olivia didn't need any other sign to get up and go. They found the energy to spring to their feet, and they began to run along the beach toward the sound. Olivia's heart was painfully fast as she ran, but she knew she had to get to the person and help them.

But when Olivia saw who was making such an anguished sound, her heart sank.

Henry…

CHAPTER TEN

OLIVIA COULD BARELY BELIEVE WHAT SHE WAS SEEING before her. What the hell was Henry Caine doing on the island? There had been no mention of him from the Gamemaster, but it definitely seemed deliberate that he was there. How could it not be?

Still coughing and spluttering from the long swim, Olivia ran to his side and checked him over for physical injuries. He was gasping for air, his face red from the heat of the sun, and he looked a little worse for wear, but otherwise unharmed. Well, other than his legs, which were still pretty heavily injured from their ordeal with ANI I. Olivia wondered how long he had been lying there unchecked, and why. Had he just woken up there? Had he perhaps been drugged and only just woken up?

Olivia checked him over thoroughly. She hadn't been able to see Henry since he was in the hospital after the explosion, and though she'd kept in contact sporadically, she hadn't heard from him in a while. Now, here he was, in the middle of her nightmares. That seemed to be the way most people came back into her life.

"Olivia… is that really you?" Henry asked, shielding his eyes from the blazing sun. "Or are you a mirage?"

"I wish I could say I was a mirage. But no. I'm really here. And we're definitely not in paradise."

Henry sat up with difficulty and threw his arms around her. She hugged him back, swallowing back tears. After everything that had happened that day, seeing Henry there, too, was almost too much for her to handle. Now that she was starting to learn the nature of the game, she knew she couldn't be too surprised. It was almost like every move the Gamemaster made was to twist the knife further into her gut.

Brock stumbled across the beach toward them and fell to his knees beside Henry, clapping a hand on his shoulder. "Hey, man. I was going to say it's good to see you… but I think given the circumstances, I'll withhold the comment. What the hell are you doing here? What happened?"

Henry shook his head. "I could ask you the same thing."

"You were in the plane crash?" Olivia asked Henry. He nodded, frowning.

"How did you know?"

"Because that's exactly why we were summoned here. This… this was no accident. It was deliberate, to put on some sick show for the rest of the world. We are being watched as we speak. Brock and I were called here because our friend Yara is here… we were told to come or else everyone would die."

"But why?"

"To play a game," Brock said solemnly. "We're being streamed live for the whole world to see, and if the FBI interferes, the Gamemaster is threatening to kill everyone—blow up the island or something. But that doesn't explain why you're involved. I'm guessing you weren't summoned here?"

Henry shook his head, his face riddled with confusion as he tried to understand what he was being put through. "I… I don't know what I've got to do with it. I thought I was just going away on a trip. I was on my way to a resort for a physiotherapy retreat for my prosthetics. An anonymous sponsor paid for my travel over there. I've been quite the hit back in England since I survived the explosion… they told me they wanted me to have somewhere incredible to recover. I didn't think too much of it… it wasn't the first gift I've received for my service. And honestly, I thought it would be a good chance to get away for a while. But I guess I was never meant to make it to the resort."

"And this was no coincidence, I'm sure," Brock said. "You were brought here to torment Olivia, to make her afraid of what she could lose here… just like Yara was brought here for me. This is starting to feel like some kind of personal attack." Brock took Henry by the shoulders. "Where are the others? Have you seen anyone?"

Henry shook his head. "I don't know… when the plane went down, there was so much chaos. I think… I think they gassed us or something to make us pass out because all I remember is waking up here a few minutes ago. I suppose if this is what you say it is, they wanted to split us up, make things more entertaining… see if we can survive on our own. I think whatever they did to us, it included some kind of muscle relaxant. I've barely been able to move. I'm dehydrated, I've just been lying here in the sun… I was only able to call out for help a few minutes ago."

"Here," Olivia said, searching in her backpack for the single bottle of water it contained. She pressed it to Henry's lips and helped him slowly drink it down, his body relaxing a little as he took in the water. He let out a deep sigh, his body shuddering in relief.

"Thank you. I owe you one, American." Henry ran a hand through his hair. "Now what, then?"

Olivia looked around them. The island was beautiful, if hell could be called that. The middle of the island was shrouded by beautiful greenery, and she could hear the chirping of insects from within the forest. She suspected that within those trees, there would be plenty of obstacles in the way of their survival, but she also knew that they had to get out of the blazing sun. The peeling skin on Henry's face was testament enough to how damaging the sun could be. Whatever waited for them within the shade would be something they'd have to deal with as it came to them.

"We should get into the shade," Olivia said decisively. "Try to rest up a little and then find some fresh water. If there is any. That would be a cruel trick if there wasn't…"

"You think there will be any?" Brock asked, raising an eyebrow. "Or do you think the Gamemaster would rather just see us die of thirst?"

"Not very entertaining though, is it?" Olivia pointed out. "There must be fresh water somewhere. But I'm exhausted from the swim. I'm going to need some time to recover. Let's get Henry out of the heat, then we can decide what to do next."

"Baby steps," Brock said with a nod. Olivia turned back to Henry.

"Do you think you can walk at all?"

Henry wavered. "I don't know. The muscle relaxant still seems to be making me feel wobbly, and I'm still getting used to my prosthetic legs…"

"I got you," Brock said, hauling Henry up from under his armpits and throwing him over his shoulder. "I still owe you one for saving my skin from ANH. It's the least I can do."

"Thanks, man. I appreciate the help."

The tired trio stumbled their way into the trees, all of them fighting against their weariness and aching bodies. Olivia was glad when they found a sheltered area to collapse in. While Brock set Henry down against a tree trunk, Olivia inspected their backpacks. Henry had drank the majority of the water they'd been given, and there was nothing but two protein bars at the bottom of the bag. Olivia presumed that the Gamemaster wanted them on the move, keeping things exciting. Which meant that even though she saw no source of food or water around them, there had to be one somewhere.

"Is that what I think it is?" Henry asked, pointing at a tree opposite them. Olivia had to squint to see what he was looking at, but it soon became clear what she was looking at.

A camera was embedded into the tree, staring right at them. It was encased in plastic and swiveling periodically to scan the surroundings. It seemed to lock onto their movements now, following them around. No doubt thousands—if not millions—of people could see them at that very moment, struggling to tend to their basic needs while they all laughed about it to themselves. It made Olivia clench her fists in anger.

"Great. Live streamed to the masses when I'm having a bad hair day," Brock groaned, flicking his wet hair off of his face. Olivia managed a small smile, but she was beginning to feel the weight of their situation. The odds were massively stacked against them. They were in unfamiliar territory, and any number of things on the island could kill them. Heatstroke, dirty water, animal attacks… and that wasn't even considering how the other survivors might act when exposed to the elements. This game was designed to make people die. Olivia wouldn't be shocked if someone had already lost their life to the game before it had even really started.

And any one of them could be next.

She felt anger bubbling beneath the surface. She wasn't just going to lie down and take her fate. Though her body ached and she still felt like she was learning how to breathe again, she refused to look weak. Somewhere out there, everyone watching was hoping they'd fail, the Gamemaster included. But she would show them. She'd show them all.

"I say we share these protein bars in our backpacks, wait until Henry is able to walk again… and then we go and investigate what we're dealing with here," Olivia said firmly. "We can't wait around too long. We're only going to get thirstier and hungrier the longer we wait. There must be some way for us to get supplies, but I'm not seeing anything obvious now. So, we need to make do with what we have."

"You're right," Henry said. "As much as I don't like it, you're right."

"Are you going to be all right? You've seen better days, pal."

"Don't you worry about me. I've survived worse than a little heatstroke and a plane crash," Henry pointed out. "Let's do this."

"Hell yeah," Brock said, glancing back at the camera. "We've got a game to win."

CHAPTER ELEVEN

THE HEAT OF THE DAY WAS BEGINNING TO WEAR ON THE trio as they trekked through the wilderness. Looking around her, Olivia could hardly believe where they were. The trees fanned out like an umbrella above her head, shielding them a little from the sun, but also trapping them in humidity and heat. Still, it was beautiful. She had never seen anywhere so green and lush. It might've been a picturesque vacation destination if not for the circumstances. But fearing for her life as well as those of the other "contestants" was going to make the next week even more difficult.

"I wish we had some concept of what time it is," Henry wheezed. He had finally been able to walk a little by himself, but the exertion seemed to be getting to him. "It feels like we've been walking for days."

"I think we've been walking for around an hour," Olivia told him. Henry shook his head.

"My fitness isn't what it was… learning to walk again hasn't exactly got me up to training standards."

"We can stop if you need to…"

Henry shook his head solemnly. "Not a chance. I'm not giving up at the first hurdle. Maybe I should see this as an opportunity to get back to peak fitness. It was supposed to be a physical therapy retreat, right? My doctors would be so pleased with me."

"That's a very positive spin on something so terrible," Brock said, glancing around them. His eyes kept finding the cameras on the trees. "How many people do you think are watching us right now?"

Olivia shook her head. "This thing will have gone worldwide. Anyone with the means to watch will be watching. People love a good show."

"I don't think anyone signed up to watch two FBI agents and an M15 guy sweating in the jungle," Henry muttered. "If we don't find water soon, we're going to be in big trouble, you know. That's what worries me most."

Olivia nodded. She was fully aware of what they were risking. She'd been listening for the slosh of running water, but hadn't heard a thing. That wasn't to say the jungle was quiet—she could hear all sorts of bugs and the scuffle of animals nearby. After the close call with the scorpions on the plane, she kept an eye on her feet. The last thing she wanted was to get stung or attacked just because she wasn't paying enough attention. It had unlocked a new fear inside her that she never expected to have.

And that wasn't the only thing joining them in the wilderness. Every now and then, a drone would fly past them, no doubt recording what they were up to. Sometimes the drone would trail them for a while, and Olivia felt oddly anxious at the feeling of being watched. She tended to be a very private person, but now the entire world was watching her every move. It was enough to unnerve most people.

Ten minutes later, they paused to sip from the bottle of water they were sharing between them. The water was warm now and did nothing to take the edge off Olivia's thirst. She knew if she ever made it home again, she would never take water for granted again.

Brock wiped sweat from his brow, shaking his head. Even as one of the fittest people Olivia knew, he appeared to be struggling. It only went to show how harsh the environment was.

"This is ridiculous. How have we been walking this long and found nothing to help us out? And where are these other 'contestants?' I thought we'd be bumping into them here, there, and everywhere. How big can this island be?"

Olivia knew he was worried about Yara. How could he not be after what he'd seen on the video of the plane going down? Olivia put a hand on his arm.

"We'll find them soon; I'm sure of it," she said. "If everyone was treated the same way as Henry, they'll be dotted all over the place. Probably to keep us all apart for a while, to watch us squirm. They're probably just getting their bearings like the rest of us."

Henry nodded. "I don't think any of the people on that plane will be very well equipped for this experience, based on what I saw of them. They're all fancy folk. I mean, they had to be to afford to get on that private jet in the first place. I bet none of them have even spent a night camping out, let alone stranded on a desert island."

"You're probably right. But there's no sense in dismissing them until we meet them," Olivia pointed out. "Who knows? They might be ready for anything. They might have some secret background that we don't know anything about."

As Olivia finished her sentence, there was a loud crackling from somewhere above their heads. It sounded like static from a speaker. Olivia looked around until she spotted a drone around twenty meters away, hovering in place.

"Good afternoon, contestants!" rang out the sinister voice of the Gamemaster. "I hope you're all enjoying the amenities of our little slice of paradise."

"It's wonderful. Best resort I've ever been to," Brock muttered. The sound of laughing came from the drone.

"Oh, Brock. I knew you'd be fun to watch. I can't wait for things to really get going so I can see how you fare. Which is exactly why you're hearing my voice now. I hereby announce that the Island Games will officially begin at the stroke of dawn tomorrow… for those of you who make it that long."

Olivia's heart skipped a beat. Had someone managed to get themselves into trouble already? Olivia wondered what horrors awaited them all on the island. But she knew she was being watched, so she kept her expression level. She wouldn't allow herself to show fear.

"Now then… I know you must all be so hungry and thirsty. I wouldn't allow my contestants to go without any sustenance for too long. It wouldn't be very entertaining to watch you all starve now, would it? So, I suggest that you all head down to the north beach where there is a welcome feast waiting for you. To those of you trekking in the jungle… it might be time to retrace your steps."

"Damn it," Henry muttered, wiping sweat from his forehead. The Gamemaster laughed again.

"Sorry about that. You'll forgive me when you see what's available at the feast. I hope you all enjoy getting to know one another… I might be back with another announcement later today. Or I might not. Who's to say?"

That chilling laughter echoed again, and the speaker cut off.

"Can't wait," Henry grumbled, already turning back on himself. "I guess we'd better get walking then."

"At least we can finish up the water," Brock said, taking it out of his backpack. Olivia shook her head.

"Maybe we shouldn't. For all we know, this is a hoax. It wouldn't be the first time today we've been played. I don't want to risk it yet."

"She's right. We should conserve it," Henry said over his shoulder, already way ahead of the other two despite the difficulty balancing on his new legs. "And don't let anyone else know we have it. If we're going to survive this, we'll need to look after ourselves first."

"Henry… we were sent here to help people," Olivia pointed out. Henry scoffed.

"I wasn't. And let's be honest; the last time I tried to help people I almost died. So, if I seem a little protective over what I have left, maybe that's why."

Olivia sighed. She had been far too quick to judge Henry for being so callous, but she understood why he was that way. She would likely be that way, too, if she had been through the experiences that he had. But it didn't change the fact that she and Brock had to help get everyone out of there alive. Henry was free to act as he pleased, but Olivia knew she would blame herself if anyone got hurt while they were on the island. She was determined to make sure that nobody had to die. And if that meant sharing everything she had, or what little she had, then she would.

The trek back to the beach was long and hard, but Olivia kept herself going with the thoughts of what might lie at the end of it. Her stomach was growling, and she could only imagine how the others must feel considering they'd gone much longer without a meal. Still the sight of food and water would definitely be welcomed, and she wasn't going to turn it down. She couldn't stop herself from daydreaming about what might be available. Some part of her was hoping for a big, juicy burger. She knew at that thought that she'd spent far too much time with Brock.

As they stumbled back onto the beach, Olivia squinted to see what was going on. Someone had set up a campfire, and there was a large table covered in food and drinks. There were already people milling around awkwardly as the sun began to set. Olivia surveyed them as she approached. Henry had been right about them—they did all look to be what he described as "fancy folk."

There were two twins standing side by side, beautiful Black women in matching white suits that would undoubtedly be completely ruined by the end of the Games. There was an older man with white wisps of hair who looked like he had never worked a day in his life. There was a grouchy woman with folded arms who seemed so snooty that she was looking down on the rest of them. Olivia swallowed. She and Brock were going to have a hard time convincing a group like this that they needed to follow their lead. They looked like they wouldn't take orders from anyone much less bother to trust one another.

Everyone was all out for themselves, it seemed.

Everyone turned to look at them as they arrived. A young man in a bright yellow shirt that he had unbuttoned to reveal his chest stepped forward to greet Henry, clapping him on the back.

"I was beginning to wonder about you, pal," he said. "Good to see you in one piece."

"Thanks, Clive," Henry said with a stiff smile. He didn't seem overly comfortable in the young man's presence, and Olivia could guess why. They didn't exactly seem like they'd have matching personalities. Clive nodded toward Olivia and Brock suspiciously.

"And who are you? You weren't on the plane."

"No, we weren't," Olivia told him. "We're with the FBI. Special Agents Olivia Knight and Brock Tanner."

That sent a chorus of murmurs through the crowd.

"The FBI is here? We're saved!"

"Are you going to get us out of here?"

"What took you so long—"

"All right, all right," Brock bellowed, his hands up to shush them. "Listen, we're in the same boat as all of you. If we can all just calm down—"

"What does that mean?" exclaimed the grouchy woman.

Olivia took a breath and tried to patiently explain. "It means we're going to do the best we can, but we're it. There's no backup coming—"

"There's no backup?"

"Why the hell would they—"

"Oh my god, we're going to die!"

"Can everyone please just *calm down?*" Brock yelled. There was still a little grumbling and moaning about it, but eventually everyone stopped panicking.

Olivia took the reins from there. "We came here by choice. We know Henry from a case we worked a while back, but that's not why we're here. The Gamemaster sent us an… invitation, so to speak. If we didn't accept, they said they would kill you all. That's the game. If we're going to do this, we need to work together. We need to learn to trust one another if we want to make it out alive."

The snooty looking woman snorted. "A likely story."

"Ignore her. Tess is very skeptical about this whole thing," the older man said with a warm smile. He stepped forward to shake Olivia's hand. "Though who can blame her when there's so much going on? I'm David."

"Nice to meet you. Wish it wasn't in such a dire situation," Olivia said.

"Um, what are we going to do?" a young woman asked anxiously, stepping forward. To Olivia's horror, she saw that the woman was heavily pregnant. What kind of monster would force a pregnant woman onto a desert island and put her through the stress of a simulated plane crash? She looked scared to death, her hair plastered to her sweaty face, and her cheeks reddened.

Olivia tried not to let her horror show as she stepped up to comfort the woman. "I don't know yet. But we're going to try our best. That I can promise you. Brock, Henry, and I have been though some terrible situations before, and we're still standing."

"Well," Henry called over. Olivia laughed despite herself.

"Well, we're still *here*," she clarified. "It takes a lot to get rid of us, I assure you. What's your name?"

"R-rose."

"It's nice to meet you, Rose. And all of you. Maybe we should all introduce ourselves?" Olivia suggested. She looked around and saw that Yara wasn't among the group. The thought made Olivia's heart seize, but there was still time. After all, they had only arrived several minutes before. Yara might be the last one to join their party.

Or so she hoped.

"Hello," one of the twins piped up, a strong French accent coming through in her voice. "My name is Elodie, and this is my sister, Clementine. Perhaps you may have heard our song on the radio."

"Oh my God. You're *Double?*" Brock asked. "You sing that really catchy song… what is it called again?"

"Racecar," Clementine supplied, tilting her chin up with a winning smile. "So, you *have* heard of us. You have good taste, clearly. I think I will like you."

Olivia scowled at the obvious display of flirting, but she looked past it to the two other young people standing close to the campfire. One was a very slim young woman with platinum hair, and the other was a man dressed all in white, looking like he was ready for a round of tennis. That's when Olivia figured out who he was—he was Harry Close, an American who had made it to Wimbledon by chance earlier that year. Henry had been right. These people were pretty well off. Harry looked up and offered Olivia a nervous smile.

"I'm Harry," he said. "And this is Melody. She hasn't said much since we got here. I think she might be in shock…"

"I'm okay," Melody murmured. "Really, I am. I'm just… taking it all in."

"It's okay to be scared. I'm scared too," Olivia admitted. "I think we would be crazy not to be. But whatever the Gamemaster plans to throw at us… if we work together, we can handle it. I promise you."

"Has anyone seen Yara Montague?" Brock asked the group. "She's an old friend of mine… she called us when the plane went down. That's how we knew to get here."

"The actress? No… none of us has seen her. We thought it might be her coming in through the forest before when you showed up," Rose said. "I hope she's okay."

Brock's shoulders sank a little, but he kept a positive smile on his face. "I'm sure she will be. She's pretty tough."

"Didn't seem tough to me," Clive said through a mouthful of food. He was standing by the buffet table, helping himself to everything. "I was sitting next to her, and she was shaking like a leaf the whole time."

"She's going through withdrawal, asshole," Melody snapped, her voice louder now. "Have some respect."

"It's not my fault she chose to be an alcoholic, is it?" Clive fired back, grinning around at the others as if they might find it amusing. Brock folded his arms, and Olivia could tell he was pleased that not one person offered a smile at Clive. He shrugged, turning back to the table, not caring that people didn't affirm him.

"I suggest you all grab a bite," Olivia said to everyone. "Who knows when we'll all see a good meal like this again?"

"I can't," Tess said, glancing at the table as if everything on it was poisoned. "I have severe allergies. Anything on that table could kill me."

Now Olivia could understand why the woman looked so sour. She was just as scared as the rest of them, but with extra anxieties. Rose stood close to Olivia, chewing her lip. She was cradling her swollen stomach.

"You don't think they'd tamper with the food… do you? I… I have to think of the baby. If any of the food isn't safe to eat…"

"We'll soon find out when Clive starts throwing his guts up," Brock said, raising an eyebrow. Olivia put a gentle hand on Rose's arm. She was clearly going to need a lot of reassurance to get through the whole experience.

"I don't think the Gamemaster would do that," Olivia responded. "It would be such a waste if all their contestants were killed before the games even began, wouldn't it? But if it makes you feel safer, we'll sample some of it first."

"How generous of you," Tess snapped. "It couldn't possibly be that you're greedy, could it? Trying to be the first at the buffet table…"

"My God, woman! You're tiring us all out with your attitude. It's not like you're jumping at the chance to try any of it," David scolded. Then he sighed, rolling his shoulders back and trying to dial back his attitude. "What are you allergic to? I'm sure we can figure out what's safe for you to eat. You won't go hungry."

Tess glared at the older man. "I don't trust your judgment. I'll take my chances and starve." With that, she walked away from the group and settled by the fire, her back to them all.

Olivia withheld a sigh. It seemed they had a group full of big characters. That wasn't going to make it easy for them all to band together. Olivia knew she needed a way to make everyone stop bickering. And what better way than to line their stomachs?

"Well, there's no sense in letting the food go to waste," Olivia said. "Why don't we all sit down… try to eat something… and we can talk about what we're going to do. We're all in this together, whether we like it or not. I'm not saying we have to be best buds with anyone here. But just… can we at least try to make it out of here?"

Slowly, but surely, with reluctant grumbles of agreement, the group gathered around the table to grab some food. And once they all started, it was hard to stop. Olivia knew that not one of them standing around the table had had to go hungry in their lives. They were lucky—wealthy and privileged beyond her wildest imagination—and now they were scrounging around for food like they'd never seen it before in their lives. Another thing to be grateful for if they made it home: access to food.

They all sat around the campfire as the sun set over the water. It was beautiful, but no one seemed to want to comment on it. Olivia understood why. In this nightmare, it wasn't a good thing. The sunset was bringing them closer to the next day and their first set of challenges. As Olivia chewed on a sandwich, she looked around the group. No one was saying much. She cleared her throat.

"Has anyone heard of the Gamemaster before? I know they have a big online following."

"Of course, we have heard of the Gamemaster," Elodie exclaimed, her French accent bright. "They offered up a million dollars to whomever could stay in a room full of cockroaches for six weeks…"

"And offered a fully-paid-for mansion to someone if they went six months without showering," Harry added, wrinkling his nose. "Made 'em do all sorts of challenges to make them sweat and then sent them out into public places to embarrass them… it was disgusting."

"It was awesome," Clive laughed. He still hadn't stopped eating, and Olivia could see all the chewed-up food in his mouth. "He's the coolest Youtuber out there. I love his content. I watch it when I'm at the gym…"

Olivia wanted to roll her eyes. She could tell that Clive was desperate to bring up the fact that he worked out.

"We don't know it's a man. That's why I don't refer to them as 'he'," Melody said quietly, glaring at Clive. He scoffed.

"Of course, it's a man. No woman could ever come up with something so interesting. You just don't want to admit that."

Olivia watched as everyone else around the campfire rolled their eyes collectively. If Clive wasn't so horrifically misogynistic, it might've been funny. At least no one else seemed interested in entertaining his backward views.

"This is a step too far, whoever is behind it," Rose said. She looked close to tears. "And I didn't sign up for this. No one in their right mind would sign up for this."

"You'd be surprised. I think the fact that the Gamemaster is so famous goes to show that people will sign up for their challenges," Elodie pointed out.

"It's true. But we're here now. We only have to survive seven days. I say we just get on with it as best as we can, and we'll be okay, I'm sure," David said. "They won't… actually kill us, will they?"

Nobody wanted to answer that. Except, of course, one man in particular.

"You've got nothing to lose, old man," Clive said, spitting food as he spoke. "You die, and at least you've lived a life. It's not like you've got many more years ahead of you. What about the rest of us?"

"You've got some nerve, kid," David said through gritted teeth.

"Please, let's not turn against each other. This is exactly what they want," Olivia said firmly, trying to divert the men away from an argument. "We just need to keep a level head on our shoulders."

"And who made you our leader?" Clive asked. Olivia gritted her teeth. He really seemed set on derailing the group.

"Nobody," she replied. "I'm just offering my opinion."

"And she's obviously right," Melody said. "She's an FBI agent. If anyone's going to keep us alive, it's her. I trust her."

"Well, there's your first mistake, kid. It's every man for himself," Clive retorted. "When the time comes, Olivia is just as likely to throw you under the bus to save herself as anyone else is."

"You're wrong," Brock growled. "Olivia has saved my life more times than I can count. She'd risk her life for any one of you. Even an idiot like you, Clive."

"I can attest to that," Henry said, looking around the group. "I wouldn't be here today without her."

"Maybe that would be a good thing. Looks like trouble follows her around, eh? She's needed to save you both multiple times, and now we're all stuck here?"

"It kind of comes with the territory when you're in this line of work," Henry pointed out. "You have to be brave and selfless. It seems like you're the only one who would have trouble understanding that."

Clive held up his hands defensively. "Whoa, easy, pal. You know nothing about me. Why the assumption?"

"I think you told me on the plane that you're a stockbroker, didn't you? I can't be sure. I wasn't really listening. Seems like you wouldn't know much about bravery and caring about others. Not really a part of your job description, is it, pal? Perhaps you should pipe down and let Olivia lead the way. All those in favor?"

Steadily, everyone around the fireplace raised their hand, aside from Clive and Tess, who was pretending like she didn't notice the rest of them there at all. Clive's face was like thunder. Perhaps he'd envisioned things going differently for him. Perhaps he thought that the women would fall desperately at his feet and the men would hail him as some kind of god. He seemed the type to feel that way, and Olivia was glad to see that he was being taken down a peg or two.

"Whatever," he said with a haughty sniff. "The day I take orders from a woman will be the day I die. If the rest of you want to put your life in her hands, then be my guest."

"Thanks so much for the permission. We were all waiting for it," Melody said snarkily, rolling her eyes. Brock smirked, glancing at Olivia with a light in his eyes. She had to admit, it was nice to see Clive's swift fall from imaginary grace, but she worried how it would affect the team overall. For now, she was just glad that most people seemed to be willing to work with her.

"I think maybe we should all fill up on food, then save some of it for the coming days. I've got a backpack we can store it in. Then we should all get some rest. Who knows what will be waiting for us tomorrow. We can all take turns sleeping. I don't know about the rest of you, but given the nature of this whole thing… I don't like the idea of no one keeping watch over us all."

The others murmured in agreement. Brock rubbed her arm gently.

"I'll keep watch with you."

"Me too," Clementine purred. "Perhaps you and I can get to know one another a little better, Brock."

"I'm not sure Olivia would be too pleased about that," Henry said with a smirk. Olivia had to hide her scowl. Clementine's flirting would get old fast. So, too, would Tess's sulking and Clive's determination to bring the group down. But they were in a better position now than when they began. They had an uneasy alliance between them all, and that was enough for her to work with for the moment. It had to be.

After around an hour, the others began to settle down. People seemed to be forming their own little groups within the group— Harry and Melody, Clementine and Elodie, Tess and Clive. David seemed to be keeping to himself while Olivia, Brock and Henry huddled together by the dying embers of the fire, keeping it stoked with some sticks they'd gathered from the tree line. Brock kept glancing into the forest, clearly wishing that Yara would show up. Olivia felt for his hand in the darkness. His skin was cool like the night air. The temperature had dropped drastically when the sun disappeared, and Olivia knew keeping warm wouldn't be easy. She was glad at least to have Brock beside her.

"She'll be okay. She's tough," Olivia murmured. Brock nodded.

"'Course she will be. But she'll be afraid."

"Join the club," Henry said glumly. "I don't like this. I don't like it at all."

"Don't give in to it. That's what the Gamemaster wants," Olivia murmured. Somewhere above them, the steady hum of a drone could be heard. Olivia tried to ignore it, but it was like the sound was in her head. There was no escaping it.

The world was watching.

CHAPTER TWELVE

OLIVIA HADN'T EXPECTED TO SLEEP, BUT THE exhaustion of the past two days had caught up to her enough to make her pass out. When she woke again, she sat up stiffly, groaning. She had sand on her face and what felt like a hundred little bug bites all over her skin. She sighed. As if she needed anything else to worry about. The environment wasn't giving her much hope for the next seven days, but she'd keep that thought to herself.

Most of the people around her appeared to be sleeping. Olivia looked around her and saw that the only few people still awake were Rose, who was standing close to the sea cradling her swollen stomach, and Henry, his eyes weary and his face defeated. Olivia shuffled closer to him and patted his arm. He jolted like coming out of a daze.

"Hey," Olivia said gently. "You doing okay?"

Henry sighed. "What do you think?"

"Well, I'd say we've both had better days… and worse too."

Henry managed a smile. "You're too jolly, American. In Britain, we don't like to see the bright side of things. It's not in our nature."

"I know. I'll never understand why so many Americans think you people are so charming. You're always bringing the mood down. You're ruining the whole vibe."

"You people?" Henry laughed quietly, and Olivia smiled. It felt nice to be back with her friend again, even under the circumstances. She hadn't been sure when she'd get to see him again. She stared out at the ocean, at Rose on the horizon, barely lit by the shimmering moonlight. She couldn't help thinking how barbaric it was that a pregnant woman had ended up there with them. She should be safe at home now, but instead she was part of a nightmare built to destroy lives, new and old.

"It adds drama," Henry said, reading her mind. "I bet the Gamemaster had her planted in this mess deliberately. I think whoever they are, they have a solid reason for choosing each of us. Like we're all here for a specific reason… we just don't know what it is yet."

"I wouldn't be surprised. Whoever this monster is… they're damn smart. They're not just manipulating us; they're puppeteering emotions. I bet whoever set this up brought you here because of me. To hurt me."

"You're probably right. Thanks for that. Much appreciated."

Olivia's expression softened. "If that's the case, then there's no chance I'm letting anyone hurt you. I'll get you out of here. I promise."

Henry tutted. "Relax, American. I might have no legs, but I'm still an MI5 agent. It hasn't dulled my senses. It hasn't taken everything from me."

"You're right. I'm sorry. I'm not trying to underestimate you. I just meant that if I'm the reason you're here…"

"I know what you meant," Henry said, running his hands through the sand beneath them. "But I don't need you to coddle me. I'm not afraid of death anymore. You and I have both looked death in the eye and told it where to go. More than once, in fact. I don't think we're the ones with reason to be afraid—at least not compared to everyone else."

"Well, I'm still afraid. Anything could happen here. And sometimes I think that escaping death once or twice only means you're not about to get lucky a third time."

"Now who's the bloody pessimist?"

Olivia smiled again. It still baffled her how far she and Henry had come. They'd once hated one another enough that they didn't trust a single word that came out of the other's mouth. Olivia had even been convinced that Henry was a turncoat working undercover for ANH. Now, she felt that despite their differences, he might be one of the few people in the world who understood her. He saw her in a way that others refused to—as the passionate, work-driven individual she was. In a weird way, she was almost glad he was there. At least he would keep her sane until they could make it home.

"You did well, keeping everyone calm earlier. That wasn't an easy task."

"Yeah, well. Someone had to try to restore some order before Clive drove everyone insane with his incessant chatter."

"You're not wrong. But I don't envy your position. They're going to be looking up to you now. You're going to need to keep up the morale," Henry said.

Olivia shrugged. "That's what I'm here for, I think. To keep everyone positive, to keep them from giving up."

He chuffed. "That's quite the task you've got then. Especially since it kind of seems like Brock isn't doing so good. I mean, you know him much better than I do, but he doesn't seem himself, does he?"

Olivia glanced at his sleeping form. Henry was right. Brock wasn't himself. He had nearly lost hope so many times when they were on the plane, when they were swimming to shore, when he realized Yara wasn't close by. Olivia knew she was watching him get pushed to his very limits. The conversation she'd had with him about finding new work partners was still fresh in her mind. She could see now why he was so desperate for an out, now that he was in a situation where everyone he cared about was under threat.

He saw his love for her as a weakness.

"He'll be okay. I think… he just needs some support to get through this," Olivia said. Henry gave her a knowing look, but didn't push the subject any further.

"I think you were right… about us all sticking together. If we do, then it might be okay," Henry murmured. Olivia nodded. That was the only solution she saw to their predicament. Teamwork and perseverance. She was tired and sore and scared, but at least she wasn't on her own. They had each other.

Olivia heard one of the nearby speakers in the trees crackle as it came to life. She looked at it warily, wondering what was going on. The moon was still high overhead, and everyone was asleep. What was the point in making an announcement at such a strange time?

"Rise and shine, my lovely contestants," the Gamemaster's voice said silkily. "I come to you with an announcement to take back to bed with you. You might want to be awake for this. I'm certain you'll all be a little more alert when I'm done speaking."

Olivia folded her arms around herself, feeling uneasy. What did the Gamemaster have up their sleeve this time? If it couldn't wait until morning, Olivia was willing to bet it was something that was going to shake things up and disturb the foundations they'd hastily built. The last thing the Gamemaster wanted was for them to work together as a team. And if tension was what the audience craved, then it was about to be injected straight into the group.

"Are you all sitting comfortably?" the Gamemaster purred. "I hope so. Because you won't be for long. There is something I failed to tell you at the start, by the way. Something important to your survival. There are twelve contestants on this island… and among you are some people you shouldn't trust. There are some of you, in this very group, that have been planted as saboteurs—imposters—to stop you from achieving your goals."

Olivia's heart sank. So much for trusting each other and working as a team.

"Which ones, you ask? Now that would be telling. And since the saboteurs aren't aware of one another… there's no way to tell who might be against you. How many are there, you ask? Only I know… and I'm not about to tell you! Ha ha ha!" Again, that shrill laughter echoed harshly. Some birds took off from the trees at the invasive noise. "So, have a good night's sleep, everyone… and let's hope no one stabs you in the back when you close your eyes. Remember… the only one you can truly trust… is yourself."

A crackle of static signaled the end of the announcement. Olivia turned to see that everyone was wide awake, looking at one another in suspicion. She pinched the bridge of her nose. This was going to be bad. How were they going to convince everyone to trust one another when the Gamemaster had dropped such a bomb on them?

"I think they're lying," Olivia said firmly. "The Gamemaster doesn't want to see us united. It makes sense that they'd try and split us all up. It's for entertainment value, not for our safety. We have to try and keep it together."

"Interesting that you'd say that…" Clive piped up, standing up from where he'd been resting on the sand, "…when you're clearly one of them."

"Excuse me?"

"You were the last to show up. You told us you were FBI, but that could be a story. I, for one, don't believe it for a second," Clive said, looking her up and down with disdain. "I mean, where's your badge?"

Olivia couldn't even begin to guess. It was likely somewhere in the wreckage of the plane or had fallen into the ocean during their swim by now.

Everyone had fallen silent. No one seemed to want to say anything that would make them look guilty, including siding with Olivia. Fingers had been pointed now, and it wasn't a good look. Olivia folded her arms.

"You were quick to point fingers, Clive. If you're trying to deflect negativity off your back, you're not doing a very good job.

I know people on this island better than you do. Brock can vouch for me, and Henry. Yara will vouch for me when we find her… that's a third of the contestants covered. I am not your enemy. And I don't intend to point fingers at *anyone*. We're in this together, and we shouldn't be trusting the Gamemaster over each other."

"What if… what if that's not true? What if there is someone out to get us?" Rose whispered. She had returned from her place by the water and was holding her stomach ever tighter. "I have to protect my baby. I won't let anything or anyone get in the way of that."

"Let's not spiral," Henry said, but Clive was already walking away across the beach.

"Where are you going?" David called after him. Clive turned on his heel.

"I'm not about to hang around here until someone decides to stab me in the back! Anyone who wants to join me can. But there's no chance I'm trusting *her*," Clive said, pointing right at Olivia. She resisted the urge to roll her eyes. She should've seen his attitude coming a mile off.

But what she didn't expect was for Elodie to follow him. Clementine grabbed her sister's arm. She began speaking rapidly in French, and the pair argued for a minute before following Clive down the beach, still bickering, both of them glancing over their shoulders anxiously. A moment later, the young tennis player, Harry, followed too. Melody tried to stop him, grabbing his arm and murmuring to him, but he didn't even look back. She didn't call after him as he left. She looked disheartened at watching her ally walk away, and Olivia felt sorry for the young girl. It was scary enough on the island without losing the person you trusted the most.

Melody glanced at Olivia with intelligent empathy in her eyes. Olivia could see that Melody was smart enough to understand what the Gamemaster was doing to them: tearing them apart until they all bled onto the sand, until they didn't know who they could rely on besides their own selves. But she had chosen not to leave, and that had to count for something.

"I trust you," she said firmly. "You're not going to let us down. And you may be right. For all we know this could all be another trick. Just something designed to tear us apart."

"I hope so," Olivia said quietly. "When all our lives are at stake, I don't see what anyone here has to gain from turning on the others. Can you imagine anyone around you turning on you? Because I can't. Nothing is certain right now, except that we all want to leave here alive. If anyone is doing anything desperate on the Gamemaster's behalf in order to survive… now is the time to speak up. I won't judge you. But we all need to be on the same side. We all need to figure this out together because whatever they've promised you, I guarantee you can't be sure that they'll follow through. You may kill and betray all of us, and then be rewarded with being betrayed yourself. So, if you have anything to admit, now is the time to do it."

The beach was quiet. Melody looked around to see if anyone would cave. David was standing with his arms folded, his age seeming to catch up to him in the moment. He seemed desperately tired and withered. Rose still seemed distraught, and Tess's sour face was now as bitter as a lemon. Their group had dwindled somewhat, but Olivia knew that this wrench in the works would change things. If she could at least keep the people on this beach safe, she would be satisfied. Clive and the others had made their own decisions. She couldn't protect them if they weren't willing to trust her.

"We should try to get back to sleep until the sun's up," Olivia insisted. "I know that was scary… but we have to keep faith in one another even more now. And we need to be ready for whatever the morning holds for us."

"I will keep watch now," David said. "I can't sleep anyway."

"Me neither," Melody said, getting to her feet. "We'll be fine just the two of us." Olivia nodded. She didn't like the idea of closing her eyes much now, but if she didn't even believe her own words, then who would? Letting her guard down would gain her more trust in the group.

She just had to hope that no one wanted her dead in her sleep.

CHAPTER THIRTEEN

WHEN OLIVIA WOKE THE NEXT MORNING, THE SUN WAS already beaming. The heat wasn't unbearable yet, but she knew it was only likely to get hotter, and it wouldn't make any of their tasks that day any easier. She had to question where on earth they were. Back home, winter was only just beginning to melt into spring, really. She would be glad when she could return to Belle Grove and escape the heat. To escape it all.

Everyone else appeared to be asleep. Melody had fallen asleep sitting next to David, and he had nodded off with his chin tilted forward. Olivia knew they really needed to stay alert, but she was glad at least that the group felt comfortable enough with each other to let their guard down. They had all made it through the first night, and that was enough to convince her that they were safe in the company they were keeping.

For now.

Olivia stretched and glanced over at the table that had been laid with their feast the night before. The uncovered food was already turning in the sun, and the waves from the water lapped at the table legs with the incoming tide. Olivia was sure it wouldn't be edible now that it had been left out. Her stomach growled, and she wished she had eaten a little more at the feast and packed more away for later. She still had a few supplies in her backpack, but she wasn't about to waste them so soon. The hunger would only get worse as the days went on, and there was no sign that the Gamemaster planned to feed them again. Perhaps they were expected to hunt. The thought turned Olivia's stomach. She had always eaten meat, but she didn't like the idea of having to kill it herself. She didn't like the thought of hurting an animal, even if that was hypocritical of her.

While the others slept, Olivia prepared herself for whatever the day might bring them. Her clothes were stiff and dry and crusted with salt from their time in the water, but she didn't have anything else to change into. She thought of the twins then in their white suits and wondered where they'd ended up with Clive and Harry. She hoped that they were all safe, despite the way they'd parted ways.

She relieved herself out of sight of the cameras (or so she hoped) and wondered again about a safe source of water to drink from and wash in. They were lucky, at least, that there was still some water on the food table. She worried about Clive's group, who had walked off without taking any with them. They would surely be dehydrated in no time. Even though they'd caused the group trouble, Olivia didn't want any harm to come to them. She thought about seeking them out and taking the water as a peace offering, but she thought it would be more trouble than it was worth. Clive would likely find some way to turn it into an act of deception on her part.

When she returned to the makeshift camp, she found Melody sorting through the food on the table. Olivia approached her and watched her sniffing at the leftover items.

"Some of it might be salvageable," Melody said with a sigh. "I wish I had eaten more. Modeling kind of means I don't get to eat stuff like this very often. And if we're going to die here, I might as well enjoy food for once in my life."

"We're not going to die here. I promise," Olivia said gently. "But hey… when we make it out, I'll take you out for a burger and a milkshake. How about that?"

Melody managed a smile. "I could get behind that. You're on." She looked Olivia up and down. "How are you doing this?"

"Doing what?"

"Managing this whole thing. You seem so calm."

Olivia could only laugh, but without any humor. "I'm not, trust me. But I'm kind of used to living life on the edge, given my job. I've been through some pretty, uh… hairy situations."

"Hairier than this?"

"You'd be surprised."

Melody shook her head. "I don't know how you do it. I would've given up a long time ago. My first instinct last night was to run away. I don't know where to, but I thought that would save me somehow. How stupid is that?"

"It's not stupid," Olivia assured her. "It's literally a human instinct. Fight or flight. It's ingrained in us."

"Yeah, well I kind of wish I was more fight than flight," she murmured.

"Well, with us by your side, we'll be able to get you in fighting shape in no time," Olivia smiled. "Today is going to be hard. Tomorrow will likely be even harder. By the end of this, we'll all be falling apart. But sticking together will keep us going. That's how I see it."

Melody sighed, turning over a limp sandwich on the table. "I hope you're right. I don't feel ready to lose it all just yet."

"Good. Because I won't let that happen."

Melody smiled shyly, and Olivia felt glad that at least one person felt comfortable around her. They spent a while sorting through the scraps of food, managing to salvage some of the unspoiled parts. They talked about finding water later that day and about what their tasks might be. But they didn't have to wonder for long. The familiar sound of the crackling speakers announced that the Gamemaster had returned to them to dole out their first task. Olivia was sure by the end of their week there she would be used to that horrible static, trained to know it meant something bad was coming their way.

If she made it that long.

"Goooood morning, my loyal fans and lovely contestants!" the Gamemaster announced cheerily. "It's a beautiful, sunny day in paradise, and it's time for you to start your first trials."

Everyone groaned and sat up, casting furtive looks around at each other.

"Somewhere on the island, there is a cache of supplies. There's food, water, weapons, and even tents to sleep in. You'll need these items if you hope to survive a week here on the island. So, your task is to find the supplies and take what you need to make a proper camp."

Olivia met eyes with Brock and nodded. There was a catch. There was always going to be.

"Simple, right? Well, be warned, the supplies are in limited stock… and you may face other challenges along the way if you want to secure the goods. And don't forget: I've got spies out to get you all… so be careful who you share your goods with. And with that, good luck—and let the games begin!"

The announcement ended, and Melody exchanged a glance with Olivia. It was clear that the announcement was made to shake them, but Olivia wanted to believe that the Gamemaster was lying to them. It wouldn't be the craziest lie she'd heard from the puppeteer in the last few days. Looking around her, she saw ordinary people who were scared out of their wits. She didn't want to believe that any of them were deceiving her or getting ready to stab her in the back. It could easily be untrue.

Still, it didn't make sense to blindly trust anyone. The only person she could truly trust was Brock. Maybe Henry, at a push, but it had been a long while since she had last seen him. He'd gone through a lot since then. Olivia knew how that could change a person, and she wouldn't rule anything out when it came to the other contestants. She wanted to believe they were all good people.

But bad situations could make villains out of them all.

Everyone had woken up for the announcement, and now they headed over to Olivia and Melody, wiping sleep from their eyes. David folded his arms and looked at Olivia for instruction.

"What do you think, Captain?" he asked a little sarcastically. "How do we proceed from here?"

Olivia swallowed. Her throat felt dry, and she could feel the heat of the sun beating down on her skin. They would quickly dehydrate in weather like this. She looked around the group.

"We have two choices, the way I see it. We can split into two groups… one can go and find the supplies and face the challenges, and the others can remain here to set up camp a little better. Rose, I know you're in no condition to be hiking for miles in this heat… I was thinking you could remain here."

"While the rest of us do the hard labor?" Tess sniffed. "Hardly seems fair."

"The woman is eight months pregnant, you imbecile," David snapped. "She's carrying a new life inside her. She has to keep it safe."

"And I suppose you'll be exempt too, won't you? Just because you're a little older? Typical," Tess sneered. Olivia chewed the inside of her cheek, trying not to lose her temper. Tess was going to be a massive issue at this rate. She didn't know why she hadn't just stormed off with Clive and the others.

"It was just a suggestion. The other option is that we could all make the trek if everyone would prefer to. We might find a water source, and we might find somewhere better to set up camp. Plus, we won't have to lug supplies back here when we find them. I'm just concerned about our more… vulnerable members. I don't want to push anyone beyond their limits."

"I don't mind making the walk," David said with a decisive nod. "I have no intention of slacking off, thank you, Tess. But you're right about Rose. She should stay here."

"I think I'll come with you," Rose said quietly. "I don't… I don't want to be left here alone. And besides, I'm not completely useless. The Gamemaster said there will be challenges along the way. I'm smart, you know. I might be able to help." She paused and smiled. "Just as long as I don't have to do any backflips, I think I'll be okay."

"If you think you can make the walk, then that's what we'll do," Olivia said with a smile. "I don't know where we should begin looking, but I say we walk through the trees. We can pace ourselves, and the shade will keep us from dehydrating too quickly. And the Gamemaster said we would find water with the supplies, so I think we can start to go through the stuff we already have. Dehydration will kill us faster than anything else, so we should keep on top of our water intake if we can."

"What a charming thought," Henry said a little groggily.

"Well, it's true. And it'll keep us going until we find the supplies."

"Assuming there are some and we're not being tricked again," Tess muttered. Olivia chose to ignore Tess. She was quickly becoming the most problematic member of the group. Olivia hoped that if they got a win that day, it would cheer her up a little. If not, she might have to say something to calm her down before she managed to scare the others.

"We might end up walking all day. I suggest that you all try and eat a little something, drink some water, and then we'll set off in ten minutes. We want to avoid the hottest parts of the day if we can," Olivia said. The group mumbled in assent and went their separate ways. Brock approached her, his eyes weary. Olivia put a hand on his cheek and looked into his eyes.

"Are you all right?"

Brock managed a small smile. "'Course I am… but there's no sign of Yara yet. I'm starting to worry about her… what if she didn't wake up from the drugs? What if she's in need of help?"

"I'm sure she's just found somewhere to camp for the night. Besides… if we're all looking for the same supplies, in theory we will cross paths. She will be looking for the same things we are. That's our best bet of finding her."

"You're right; you're right. Thanks for keeping my feet on the ground."

"Well, I wouldn't just let you float away from me, would I?"

Brock smiled for real this time, and Olivia gave him a light kiss. She had almost forgotten that they were being watched worldwide. She blushed and moved away from him. The last thing she wanted was to put on a romantic display for millions of streamers to see. She had no intention of giving the audience anything they actually wanted. She was there to survive, not to entertain the viewers.

It took longer than ten minutes for the group to get themselves together, but Olivia was pleased that once they got going, they all managed a decent pace. Even though Rose was a little slower than the rest and wanted to stop occasionally, she was doing her best given her condition, which was all anyone could ask for. Rose put on a brave face, not wanting to seem a burden, but everyone's sympathy for her caused them all to take regular breaks which kept them from burning out. It turned out to be a good thing.

Olivia knew that it was important for them to find the supplies fast. She wouldn't put it past Clive to steal everything for himself if he got there before they did. But she also knew she had to be mindful of the rest of the group, and her own body was still sore from the events of the previous day. She saw no sense in wearing them all out before they even reached their destination.

Even in the shade, though, the heat of the day could be felt. Olivia had sweated through her shirt in no time. Within the first two hours of the trek, the others began to tire, and as far as Olivia could tell, they were no closer to their goal. It was impossible to know where the supplies could be since the island was a maze they'd never explored before. But they pressed on, heading in one direction and hoping it would yield prizes for them all.

They stopped for a while so Rose could sit down, and they all shared some water and the leftover food. Then Olivia insisted that they push on. She didn't want to lose anyone to the elements, but their mission was crucial. There was no denying that they needed the supplies, and the worn-down group also needed a win for the sake of their morale. Nobody complained as they continued on, not even Tess.

In the third hour, Olivia was getting tired herself. Her skin was itching from insect bites, and her muscles were tight and sore. She wasn't about to complain out loud, but the others were slowing down, and she knew they would have to give up sooner or later. It was becoming clear that they were running out of steam.

But then, Olivia spotted something ahead through the trees. Her eyes widened. There was a pile of supply boxes straight ahead, piled up like a precarious tower. She tried not to let her relief show on her face. She had no idea what was in the boxes, but she knew they had found where they were supposed to be. It had to be the right place.

"Guys… I think we found them," Olivia said, wiping sweat from her upper lip.

"About bloody time," Henry panted. "Let's get over there and sit down. We can all rest up and dole out the supplies."

"Hang on… where's the challenge?" Melody said cautiously. "The Gamemaster said there would be a challenge… surely it won't be as easy as walking up and taking what we want?"

"We can go and investigate," Olivia said, already leading the way. She could see now that there was something in front of the supply crates. It only became clearer what it was when they got closer.

There were six rows of four tiles presented in front of them. Each tile appeared to have a symbol carved on it. The symbols didn't give much away. Some of them were abstract shapes, and others resembled animals or inanimate objects. In front of the tiles stood a podium with several note cards on it. Olivia turned to the group and waved the cards at them.

"Looks like this is the challenge here," she said.

Henry rubbed his hands together. "All right. Read it out. Let's see what we're dealing with."

Olivia took a closer look and read the first card out loud as slowly as she could.

"*I speak without a mouth and hear without ears. I have no body, but I come alive with wind. What am I?*"

"What are you talking about?" Tess snapped from behind her. "That doesn't make any sense."

"It does make sense. We just have to make sense of it. It's a riddle," Melody said. She stood beside Olivia and examined the tiles before them. Olivia could see a featureless head on one tile, three pairs of curved lines which got bigger as they expanded outwards, a thundercloud, and a snake. Olivia took it all in and began to understand what the task was.

"We have to pick the right path to the supplies," Olivia murmured. "Solve the riddles one by one and take the stepping stones up to the supplies."

"Very good," the Gamemaster's voice appeared from a nearby speaker. "Nothing gets past superstar federal agent Olivia Knight, now does it? You have no time limit for this task, since I'm feeling generous. But be warned… one misstep could be fatal. Fun, right?"

Olivia wanted to tell the Gamemaster to shove it, but she resisted. Olivia examined the stepping stones again, trying to think of an answer to the first riddle. None of them really made any sense just by looking at them. She figured they'd have to solve the riddle first and then pick a tile after that made sense with the answer. It was the most logical way of approaching it.

"Let me read that again," Melody said, examining the card. "I speak without a mouth and hear without ears… I have no body… what about the picture of the head? It doesn't have ears or a mouth, and it definitely doesn't have a body…"

"I mean, yes, from a physical standpoint you're right… but I don't think it makes sense as an answer to a riddle. What's that got to do with wind?" Olivia pointed out.

"Well, we don't have a time limit," Henry said as he slumped down against a tree behind them, looking a little red in the face. "I say we take our time and think the answers through properly."

"Agreed," Melody said. "But it looks like I might not be the best person for this job…"

"I like riddles," Rose said quietly from behind them. She was cradling her stomach again, resting beside Henry. "Give me a few minutes to think… I'll come up with an answer."

"Well, what do we have here?"

Olivia turned to see that Clive was coming through the trees with Harry, Clementine and Elodie in tow. He wore a cocky grin as he surveyed the puzzle before them. Olivia's stomach twisted. The last thing they needed was competition.

"We have to solve the riddles to get to the supplies. Would you like to join us and work together?" Olivia asked as politely as she could muster. Clive scoffed at her.

"Yeah, right. Like I'd work with you. What is this garbage, anyway? Looks like hopscotch for kids."

"We have to pick the right path to the supplies based on the riddles," Olivia said, choosing to ignore Clive's rude comment toward her. He shook his head and chuckled to himself.

"What a load of crap. You seriously expect me to go through all that? The supplies are right there!"

"But—"

"It's a test of courage, Olivia. Something you might not understand," Clive sneered, standing in front of the puzzle and rolling his eyes at it. "We should just walk up and take what we want. Show the Gamemaster what we're made of. He'll love that."

"Clive, don't—"

Before anyone could stop him, Clive walked over the first set of tiles and stepped onto the second. For a moment, nothing happened. He turned to give Olivia a smug grin, as if to say, *I told you so.*

And then the bullet went through his skull.

CHAPTER FOURTEEN

Tess and Rose screamed as Clive crumpled to the ground before them. Olivia's eyes were wide with shock, looking around for the sight of the gunman. She spotted a man with a sniper perched in a tree and felt her blood boiling. They'd been told there would be obstacles... but not like this.

Clive shouldn't be dead. He was a jerk, but he didn't deserve to be treated like this. No one did.

"Everyone—everyone, stay back," Olivia stammered, trying to gain some control over the situation. The last thing they needed was anyone else getting hurt. She was burning with anger: with Clive for wasting his own life, thinking he knew best—with the Gamemaster for putting them in this position in the first place—with the rest of the world for watching this unfold as though their lives meant nothing… like this was all some Hollywood movie. It was sick.

And now a man was dead.

"I told you all to follow the rules…" the Gamemaster's omnipresent voice spoke. "You *must* solve the puzzle. No one may touch those supplies until the last riddle is solved. You saw what happened to our friend Clive. If anyone wants to follow him into death… well, be my guest. Doesn't matter to me."

Melody grabbed Olivia's hand, trembling; Clementine and Elodie were clutching each other; and the others were all watching in horrified silence. The sound of the shot was still ringing in Olivia's ears. How were they supposed to come back from this now? It had shattered the illusion that they might be safe there. That they could just quietly solve the riddles in their own time and get a win.

It was a fatal game, and they couldn't afford to forget it.

"It's okay," Olivia murmured. "We're going to follow the rules now. We're going to solve the riddles… and everything will be fine."

"Fine? Clive's gone!" Harry cried, panic in his voice. He was trembling where he stood, staring at Clive's still body. His blood was starting to soak onto the tiles.

"You may have five minutes to get Clive away from the scene. Someone will be by to pick up his body," the Gamemaster told them in a low voice. "But now I grow impatient. A time limit will now be put in place. You have an hour to solve the puzzle before I let my sniper get trigger-happy. You were warned. This is your punishment."

Olivia was furious. If she had weapons available to her, she would take that sniper down in a heartbeat. But she didn't know what else lurked on the island… what else waited for them. She suspected that the Gamemaster wouldn't allow three seasoned agents onto the island without suitable forces to subdue them. If there was one sniper they could see, there might be ten other gunmen that they couldn't, waiting for any excuse to shoot them down. Olivia had no doubt that the Gamemaster would make good on their promise. After all, the "contestants" had all come here to die, if the Gamemaster got their way.

The Gamemaster's voice faded out once again. Tess let out a strangled sob, and Olivia stared at Clive for a few moments, not knowing how to fix the mess they'd been presented with. How were they supposed to come back from this? How were they supposed to concentrate on riddles when a man had just died right in front of them? Everyone was panicked and upset. It was a terrible environment for teamwork.

"We have to keep going," Olivia said, turning to the others. "It's awful, I know. I don't like it any more than you do. But we have to keep going. We can mourn later. But if we don't make a move… we're all going to die. You heard what the Gamemaster said. And we've seen what happens when people don't follow the rules."

"You're right," Melody said, her voice raspy as she held back tears. "Clive made a bad choice. Let's not follow in his footsteps."

"Should we move him?" Harry asked, casting a glance at Brock. He nodded.

"Okay. Let's get him off the tiles."

Brock and Harry tentatively approached the tiles. Olivia held her breath, half expecting them to get shot down for their efforts, but they safely lifted Clive's lifeless body up and began to carry him away. Olivia had to look away. She'd seen plenty of dead bodies in the course of her career… but knowing that a man had died for no reason other than his own foolishness? That there was no reason he had to die? That was a hard pill to swallow.

And now he had put the rest of them at further risk. The time limit in place added much more pressure to the situation. Olivia wasn't afraid of a challenge, and she was no stranger to problem solving; but as she looked at the symbols in front of them, she realized how vague they were. It would be easy to pick the wrong tile even if they knew the right answers. She swallowed. She couldn't afford to be tentative now. The team needed her to take the lead.

"I speak without a mouth and hear without ears. I have no body, but I come alive with wind. What am I?" she repeated out loud. Melody stood close to her, her mouth moving as she repeated the riddle silently to herself.

"An echo."

Olivia turned to see Rose standing close by, her hand cradling her belly. Her face was stained with silent tears, but she looked determined.

"An echo?"

"Yes. It's not a physical entity… but it creates sound without a mouth, and it listens to what a person is saying without ears to repeat the noise. Does that make sense?"

Olivia considered it and nodded. "Yes… yes, it does," she replied. "And it comes alive with wind. An echo. That must be it, Rose. Good job."

Harry and Brock returned silently from taking Clive's body away. Everyone fell into horrified silence. They had so quickly pushed what happened aside, but did they have any other choice? When it came to survival, Olivia knew they'd all do anything to make it through. Even if it meant acting callous for a little while. She swallowed and turned back to the tiles.

"So, we have our answer. Now we have to pick the tile to stand on. I guess one of us is going to have to pave the path. Step on the tiles to pick our answers."

"Well, it doesn't sound like you're volunteering, FBI," Tess snapped, glaring at Olivia. Olivia frowned.

"I'll do it. I'm happy to," she said firmly. She had no interest in impressing Tess, or trying to get on her good side, but she knew that backing down from this particular challenge would cause the group to lose confidence in her. Besides, she'd gone there with the mission of saving lives. If she took a misstep and took a bullet for her trouble, then at least she would save someone else from that fate.

But someone immediately took issue with that fact. Olivia knew he would.

"No," Brock said, shaking his head fervently. "If you make one wrong step, you're dead, Olivia."

"The same applies to anyone," Olivia said coolly. "Have some faith, Brock. I'm not going to make any wrong steps. Don't you trust me?"

Before he could argue further, Olivia stepped up to the tiles, trying to ignore the fact that Clive's blood was still soaking into the ground before her. She took a deep breath and checked out the tiles.

"I think it must be the curved lines. They must represent the echo getting louder, right? It's certainly not the head or the thunderclouds. I don't see what a snake has to do with anything. It feels like the only one that makes sense, if the answer is right." She swallowed. She didn't want to sound uncertain, but knowing that a wrong step could kill her was scary enough. Still, she'd volunteered. There was no going back now.

"So? What do we think?"

"Yes," Rose said firmly. "I'm right. I'm sure of it."

"Are you? Because if you're wrong, her head goes *ker-plewie*," Tess said, her words dripping with venom. Olivia resisted the temptation to scowl and shook her head.

"Tess, please. That's not helpful. And I trust Rose's judgment. It sounds right to me. And if we don't make quick work of this, more people will get hurt. I'm going to do it."

Tess huffed. "Your funeral."

Olivia blocked Tess out again. She didn't hesitate as she stepped onto the first tile, despite the fluttering of anxiety in her stomach. She waited tensely for something to go wrong, for the sound of a bullet ripping through the air, but nothing came. She tried not to let her relief show on her face. She needed to put on a good front so she didn't spook the others.

"All right… I guess we made it through the first one," Olivia said with a shaky laugh. "Melody… can you read out the next one?"

Melody stepped up to the podium where Olivia had just been standing, clearing her throat anxiously. Her eyes scanned over the words. *"Whoever makes it has no need of it. Whoever buys it has no use for it. Whoever uses it can neither see nor feel it. What is it?"*

Olivia frowned and looked at the next set of symbols. They were still a little ambiguous. One of the images was a hand, and another was an eye. But the other was an unusual, oblong shape, and the final tile had an image of a heart.

"A heart… I guess if that's a symbol of love, then the person who makes it has no need of it? It's something you give," Rose mused.

Melody shook her head. "That sounds like overthinking it. And I would argue that whoever uses it definitely does feel it. So no, not love."

Olivia listened to the others deliberating, but she had her eyes on the oblong shaped symbol. It took her a few moments to realize what it was supposed to represent, but as soon as it became clear, she knew it was the right answer. She stepped forward boldly and the others cried out as though to stop her, but she was certain in her choice. Silence filled the air as she stood firmly on the second tile.

"It's a coffin," Olivia said quietly. "The person who builds a coffin doesn't use it. Someone buys a coffin for you after you die, but they have no use for it. And when you're dead… well. You don't see or feel."

Clive's death hung heavy in the air. Olivia knew there was no chance he had expected to die at his age. He was so young. He wasn't prepared for it. He thought he was invincible, untouchable by anything life threw at him.

He'd been proved so wrong so quickly.

And he'd died alone in such a strange place, away from home, away from a place where he knew love and care. Olivia's heart squeezed. She had no idea what kind of life Clive had back home, but it felt like that didn't matter much. Everyone had someone waiting for them, loving them. Someone was probably crying over him now, crushed by his death. She hoped the Gamemaster would make sure he got home. That was the least they could do for their fallen contestant.

"This is good," Henry said encouragingly. "You ladies are smashing these answers. But don't forget, we're on a time limit."

Olivia nodded. It was impossible to know how much time they had left, and although she felt she was moving quickly, she had no idea how much harder the questions would get. She couldn't risk getting stuck on one question. She suspected she might have to make a few leaps of faith.

"Next one?"

Melody cleared her throat once again. "Okay… here goes. *You measure my life in hours, and I serve you by expiring. I'm quick when I'm thin and slow when I'm fat. The wind is my enemy. When I'm alive, we sing; when I'm dead; we clap our hands. What am I?*"

"God damn," David muttered. "What kind of question is that? There's way too much to consider."

"Nope," Rose said. "I know this one. It's a birthday candle. When it's alive, we sing happy birthday. When it's dead, it's been blown out by the birthday boy or girl. Wind would blow it out, and it burns quicker when it's a thin candle."

"You're on a roll, girl," Melody said with a warm smile. Olivia could feel her heart slowing a little. It seemed like they had it in the bag. She easily picked out the right symbol and moved forward. There were only three questions left, and they would have all the supplies at hand.

"*What can go through glass without breaking it?*" Melody asked, but before anyone could answer, she shrugged. "Easy. That's light."

"You're getting cocky," Tess snapped at her. "How can you be so sure?"

"Tess, what else do you know that goes through glass without harming it? It's not a difficult question," Melody said, folding her arms. "We just have to pick the right symbol."

Olivia checked the next row in front of her. The symbols were once again harder to work out than the answers. Two of them were easily discounted: a fist and a water symbol. But one image seemed to show light waves, another a lightbulb. Olivia felt like the lightbulb wasn't specific enough for it to be right, and yet it did depict a source of light. The other symbol was very abstract.

"What do you think? Abstract or lightbulb?" Olivia asked the group. She wanted to be sure of her steps this time.

"The lightbulb doesn't seem accurate enough," Clementine said, chiming in for the first time. She had a guilty look on her face, and Olivia knew she was thinking about the fact that she and her sister had run off with Clive at the first opportunity. It was almost like she was trying to make up for what had happened. "I think it must be the other one."

The group murmured their agreements. Brock looked pale and unsure, but Olivia chose to ignore that. She understood his anxiety. She was taking her life in her hands with this dangerous game. But someone had to walk the path, and she had to make a decision. Taking a deep breath, she veered away from the lightbulb and onto the correct tile.

Olivia let out a long sigh of relief. Another safe spot. There was just one final row to go. If it remained as simple as the rest of the questions, then it might be okay. They might make it out alive. But nothing was guaranteed. Nothing was that simple.

And especially now, she worried, maybe they had been lulled into a false sense of security.

She took a steadying breath as Melody prepared to read the last question. Olivia kept her expression neutral. She knew thousands of people were watching to see how she would respond to the trials she was facing. She wasn't going to give them a single shred of satisfaction, no sense of entertainment. That was what they wanted, and she was angry about it. No, she would make it through, and she would do it with a stoic expression.

"*What gets broken without being held?*" Melody asked the group. Everyone fell into silence as they considered the answer. The symbols before Olivia were simple enough. A blank tile, a heart again, two pinky fingers interlocking, and a wine glass. Olivia was sure it wasn't the wine glass. That didn't make any sense to her.

But the others… they were tricky. A heart could easily be broken, and you couldn't physically hold it. The interlocked fingers made Olivia think of promises… another thing that could be broken without being held. She didn't know what the blank tile represented, but she felt drawn to it, wondering what it could mean.

"What about silence?" Rose offered. "You can break silence, and you don't hold it."

"That's good," Melody said, giddiness in her voice. "I don't know how you're doing this, Rose."

"But wait," Olivia said, pointing to the symbols. "Promises and hearts both fit too. I guess the blank tile could represent silence… but then it feels like it could be any of those three answers. How are we meant to pick between them all?"

Silence fell upon the group as they considered what she was saying. *If only we could break this silence now,* Olivia thought. She knew she had presented them with a conundrum. There could only be one true answer, but all of them could be right. It made the game feel so much more dangerous. They could discount the wine glass, yes, but they still had a one in three chance to get it right. Those odds didn't feel good to Olivia.

"What do we do? We have to pick one!" Elodie said, wringing her hands tightly. Olivia turned back to the tiles. She was right, but she was also wrong. They didn't need to pick.

She did.

One misstep, and she was dead. But at least the odds would be better if she got it wrong. Someone else could take a shot at the right answer.

The only thing it would cost her was her life.

"Olivia… don't do anything rash," Brock's voice of reason sounded behind her.

"I'm going to have to at some point," Olivia replied. "We're running out of time."

"We still have some time to think it over…"

"It's an impossible question, Brock. Three of the answers make sense. But each of them could be wrong. I need to move soon so there's a second opportunity for someone to get it right before time runs out."

"You are *not* sacrificing yourself!"

Watch me, Olivia thought. She knew one thing for certain: if she had to trade her life to get the others to the end of the island, she would. That was her job. But she had to have faith in herself. She had made missteps in life before, but never ones that got her killed. There was a first time for everything, but she knew herself. She knew she was led by her gut, and her gut was telling her that Rose was right— silence had to be the answer.

She hesitated for a single moment—was she doing the right thing?—before she made her leap of faith. As soon as her feet hit the empty tile, her entire world seemed to stop. Her heart stopped beating, her lungs failed to work, her ears blocked out the cries of the contestants. She closed her eyes and accepted whatever her fate might be.

And nothing happened.

She opened her eyes again. The bounty was now close enough to touch. She stepped up to it and touched the supply boxes. And still nobody shot at her. Nobody tried to hurt her.

She'd won.

She breathed; it was like she'd been holding her breath for years, and the terrified cries of her teammates turned into applause. They'd made it. They had done the impossible. Olivia tried not to allow her face to crumple in relief. She couldn't let up now. She had to look strong—look capable. She looked up at the sky, wondering if the Gamemaster had enjoyed the show.

"Congratulations. Enjoy your bounty. I'll be back tomorrow with your next task," the voice said, sounding bored. Olivia smirked. She gathered that the Gamemaster expected them to die, to make a wrong turn.

But they'd made it through step one. They just had six more to survive.

CHAPTER FIFTEEN

OLIVIA COULDN'T BELIEVE THEY HAD MADE IT THROUGH the first task. After the last impossible question, she felt lucky to be alive but also angry that she felt that way. She shouldn't have to be grateful that she'd been spared to live another day. The task was won thanks to her. Because of her, no one on the island would starve that week. But they wouldn't have to worry about that if they hadn't been forced to be there in the first place. It didn't feel like a victory when the only prize was their survival for another day.

Still, at least they wouldn't go hungry or thirsty now. At least there would be no more sleeping out on the sand. The entire group was sitting around in a circle. After the task was done, Melody and Harry had helped her pitch the tents while Brock and

David sorted through the supply crates. Now, they were feasting on some of the snack bars they'd found inside the boxes. Tess still hadn't touched anything, but everyone else seemed pleased with what they'd found.

It should've been enough to keep them sane. But tensions were high.

Everyone was thinking about what had happened to Clive, and there was still a massive elephant in the room—the saboteurs. With Clive gone, it narrowed down the people they could trust even further. It didn't help that the remains of Clive's group had rejoined them, sitting separately from the others as though they might still turn on them. Olivia had already tried to get the twins talking, and Melody had tried to rekindle the friendship she seemed to have formed with Harry, but the trio remained somber and untrusting. It made sense on some level, but it was also ridiculous to think about. They were willing to feast on the supplies Olivia's group had won for them, but they wouldn't eat together? As if the three of them had any reason to trust one another more than the others?

Olivia knew that these divisions would be the death of them. It was hard enough trying to get through this without everyone being against one another. Olivia had thought their victory in the first task might have been enough to keep them all on good terms, but apparently not. If she didn't do something soon, she was concerned it would all fall apart again.

Olivia stood up slowly, and all eyes were drawn to her. She clasped her hands in front of her, trying not to look as nervous as she felt.

"I thought maybe I would take five minutes to go and quietly pay my respects to Clive on the beach," she announced. "Would anyone like to join me?"

"I think that's a lovely idea," Rose said immediately, standing up with some difficulty. Tess scowled at Olivia.

"He didn't even like you. He said you were one of the spies."

"He was wrong. That's not a crime," Olivia said plainly. "And I don't hold it against him. We're all under a lot of pressure here.

We're not our best selves right now. So, I want to ensure he's remembered well, as he should be."

"I'll come," Brock said.

"And me," Henry added as Brock helped him to his feet. "I'm supposed to get a few minutes of light walking every day anyway. Doctor's orders."

Olivia couldn't help but chuckle at that. "And that horrible trek all morning wasn't enough?"

He shrugged. "Technically it was a hike. Not exactly light walking."

She smiled. "Great. Maybe we can walk down to the water, now that the evening is cooler."

The four of them set off for the edge of the ocean. Olivia was glad for some time away from the large group. It was becoming more difficult to keep her temper in check when some were so argumentative. She felt Brock's hand on her shoulder and sighed against his touch.

"You doing okay? You really saved our asses today," Brock whispered to her. She smiled.

"Well, I can't say it did wonders for my blood pressure. But I'm okay. I'm just glad it worked out. For the most part, at least."

"So am I. But I didn't doubt you. I knew you'd make the right decision. You always do. I hope you didn't think I didn't have faith in you. I just didn't want you in harm's way."

"Thank you, Brock."

"And…" He looked away for a moment, seeming to gather his thoughts. "Well, I just wanted to apologize for being so on edge earlier. Not that I'm not still pretty stressed now," he admitted with a chuckle. "I've been seeing only the worst outcomes, only focusing on the negatives, when I should be just trying to get us out of here as best as I can. You were right—the way you always are. So, just… thanks for being patient with me."

Olivia blushed. A strange thought crossed her mind—were the people at home watching them *rooting* for her and Brock? She'd watched enough reality TV in her life to know that there were always fan favorites. The ones people loved, the ones they formed attachments to. She didn't expect to be one of them, but she wondered if their love story might inspire the watchers to at least want them to survive. It was crazy that she even had to think about that. But if it kept her alive a little longer, if it meant the Gamemaster was kinder to them… then maybe it wasn't such a bad thing. If love was the only card she had to play, she would play it every chance she got.

Then an even stranger thought crossed her mind—were her parents watching? She imagined that they wouldn't be able to look away. An event of this magnitude wouldn't just be live streamed; it would be televised as well. She was sure that people all over the world were tuning in to see what would happen to the twelve people trapped on an island.

Eleven now, Olivia thought. Ten, if they assumed Yara was dead. A chill ran down her spine. She didn't want to believe it, but her absence was starting to worry Olivia. If she was on the island, why hadn't they crossed paths with her yet?

"Where do you think she is?" Brock asked, reading her mind as they reached the edge of the water. Rose and Melody were giggling together as they padded along the shore, their cares forgotten for a short time. Olivia sighed.

"I wish I knew. I thought… I thought she would've met us here. She must have heard the messages, right? I thought she would've made it by now. It almost feels like she can't possibly be looking for us. It's been too long."

"I thought the same. I just… I just don't want to believe it. I… I just want some answers."

"Well, let's not give up just yet. Maybe she will surprise us," Olivia said softly. She glanced at the other two women, who had quickly sported guilty looks on their faces for enjoying themselves. Olivia felt sorry for them. Both of them seemed like ordinary, kind young women. They didn't deserve to be there— none of them did—but perhaps those two least of all. Olivia cast a glance at Rose's swollen stomach and wondered how anyone could be so cruel as to put her through such an ordeal. It made her feel sick.

"Should we have a moment of silence?" Rose said with a sad smile. It was such a gentle and kind thought that it brought Olivia right back to the present. Olivia nodded.

"That sounds nice."

Olivia's hand found Brock's, and the whole group fell silent as they said their goodbyes to Clive. Olivia hadn't liked the man much. He was reckless and sexist and determined to fling his crap into everyone else's faces. But Olivia didn't believe he deserved to die—not for that. They would never, ever have been friends, but his life should never have ended in such a brutal, horrific fashion. For better or worse, she would never forget him. And she hoped that whatever came after death, it was peaceful for him.

When Olivia opened her eyes again, Rose was wiping tears from her face. Melody put an arm around her and led her away from the water.

"Come on. It's all right. You're safe."

The group trudged back to the camp together. Olivia felt a little better now, knowing that she had given the group a chance to grieve and make space for the hurt inside them. She couldn't imagine how hard it would be if they lost anyone else. She wanted so desperately for everyone to make it out of there alive, but Clive's stunt had proven that might be impossible. She only hoped there wouldn't be any further incidents.

Back at the camp, Olivia looked around and realized that the group was a little smaller. Then she saw Clementine and Elodie shooting guilty glances in her direction. She frowned, trying to pinpoint who was missing. She frowned.

"Where's David?"

Clementine stood up, looking anxious. "I tried to stop him… but he ran off before I could chase after him. He… he took a bunch of supplies and left. I'm so sorry…"

Olivia felt her stomach twist. She should've known that things would fall apart like this. She rubbed her forehead and let out a heavy sigh. She wouldn't have guessed that David would be the one to let the group down, but she knew she should really learn to expect the unexpected. He must've gotten scared and thought he'd be better off alone. She looked around at the rest of the group. There were frightened and frustrated faces among them. They were expecting her to say something, to come up with a solution for his treachery. But she had no real power here. No way to enforce law.

She would just have to let him get away with it.

"Whatever he took, it can't have been enough to truly affect our supply. He can barely carry himself, let alone the supplies," Olivia finally said, earning a chuckle from Melody. "It sucks, but he's made his own choices. We can manage with just us. He's on his own now. Come tomorrow, I'm sure he will regret that."

"Are you threatening him, FBI?" Tess asked, her mouth falling open. Olivia turned to her.

"Of course not. I'm just saying that we all have each other's backs here. When the task is announced in the morning, I think he will come to his senses. Maybe he'll come back. Maybe he will realize he's made a mistake."

"And you'll allow that to happen?" Elodie asked with a raised eyebrow. Olivia shrugged.

"That would be up to the group. But it's like I said. We're not our best selves right now. Logic has gone out of the window. Maybe it would be best if we didn't judge each other too harshly," Olivia said, keeping her voice level. "Besides… you, your sister, and Harry only rejoined our group today. If we're willing to look past what happened between us all, then can't we extend the same offer to David?"

The others began to mutter among themselves. She had to admit, David's betrayal hurt, and she wasn't happy about it. But did she blame him for running scared? Not really. There were worse things he could've done. She felt it was definitely something she could move past. It wasn't like he'd screwed the entire group over by taking a small set of supplies.

"But maybe this isn't the end," Tess said darkly, desperate to turn the mood once again. "He could've been one of those spies. What if he has more planned for us? What if he sneaks back into camp at night and finishes us off, one by one?"

The comment sent a chill down Olivia's spine. She didn't want to think about that. Somehow, she didn't see how that could happen. David was a nice enough man, and an older gentleman. Olivia didn't see him doing such horrible things. But the prospect was chilling. She knew she was there to try to save these people—to help them if she could—but what if they didn't want saving? What if she was trying to save people who were plotting against her behind her back? What if the real game was that the whole island was against her, Brock, and Henry? What if they were playing the long game, convincing her she was safe before they struck her down? Perhaps that was why Yara had never shown up. Maybe they'd taken care of her first.

Olivia blinked several times, fanning away the thoughts. She was being paranoid, and she knew it. She needed to keep her feet firmly on the ground. If she let her thoughts run away with her, then she'd never make it to the end.

"That's not going to happen. I won't allow it," Olivia said firmly. "Brock, Henry, and I are going to keep you all safe to the best of our ability. But if we want this to work, we have to be more careful. You saw what happened to Clive today. You saw how David took matters into his own hands. We don't have the power here, but we can control our environment. So that means looking out for one another. We have to commit to not allowing panic to change things between us, no matter how hard it gets. Understood?"

Everyone in the group nodded solemnly. Even Tess sighed and nodded her agreement. Olivia had to see that as progress.

"I don't think it's going to get any easier for us," Melody said quietly. "Today was child's play. I think the true challenges will begin tomorrow."

CHAPTER SIXTEEN

O LIVIA WAS AWAKENED THE FOLLOWING DAY BY THE blazing sun and the fear in her own heart. She was glad at least to be inside a tent next to Brock and Henry, away from the prying eyes of the cameras. She sat up and stretched, anxiety gnawing at her stomach. Another day meant another task, and there were still so many questions unanswered. Why were they all there? Would any of them get out of there alive? Would they ever find Yara?

She wondered how the world was reacting to the death of the first contestant. Were they as saddened as the other islanders, knowing that a man lost his life for no reason? Or were they eager to carry on watching, sitting on the edge of their seats, reveling in the carnage and spectacle while the Gamemaster made a mockery of them live on the internet? Olivia didn't want to believe that the second option was more likely, but she was sure it was.

Olivia rubbed at the back of her neck. If anything, her body ached more now than it had the day before. Exhaustion was setting in after pushing her body to its limits. But she couldn't afford to let weakness take over her body. There would be a new task soon, and Olivia would have to lead the team through it if they hoped to live another day. They would be relying on her more than ever now that they'd seen how scary the island could truly be.

The two men were still sleeping, so Olivia crawled out into the camp. Melody was sitting on a felled log, keeping watch. Olivia went and sat down beside her. She had found a kinship with Melody in their short time together. She was a sweet girl who clearly had a level head on her shoulders, and she seemed like she liked Olivia too. She had to admit she liked her company more than most of the others, and it felt easy to talk to her, to reason with her. She was sure they'd become a good team in their time together.

"Have you been on watch for long?" Olivia asked Melody. She shrugged.

"I'm not sure how long. A couple hours maybe. No one else wanted to do it, so I just let them all sleep. I can't face going to bed."

"You have to keep your energy up, too, you know. You'll be exhausted."

"Oh, I know that. I have insomnia. This is like my bread and butter. Not that I've had bread or butter in a long time."

Olivia laughed. "Brock would be distraught if he heard you say that. Bread and butter *is* his bread and butter. Especially if you add a burger patty on top."

Melody smiled back. "I can't argue with that. You know… I think I might quit modeling when I get home. It seems there may be more to life than staying skinny and pouting for cameras. Namely cheeseburgers."

Olivia laughed. "Oh, I don't know. Being beautiful has its benefits."

"I guess it does. But that too will disappear someday. Everything good does with time," Melody said in a dark tone.

Then she quirked a smile to let Olivia know she was joking. "I never really intended to be a model, but I kind of fell into it. I knew a guy who knew a guy who… well, it paid the bills. And then it started paying the bills on a three-floor mansion in LA, and who was I to turn that down? I didn't mind the travel, the perks, the lifestyle either. I thought, *Hey… law school can wait.* And it just slipped into the back of my mind, I guess."

"It could still be waiting. There's nothing stopping you."

Melody's smile was a little sadder this time. "Maybe. I don't know. I guess you never do know where life will take you. I certainly never expected to be where I am now…"

Olivia's heart squeezed. Here Melody was, pouring her heart out, and now people all over the world would see her at her most vulnerable. Maybe she was used to that in the modeling industry, but it felt wrong. She shouldn't have to share those thoughts with anyone but the person she was talking to. Melody glanced upward at the rising sun.

"Anyway. I guess we have to get through all of this before I can think about going to school. What do you think they'll have us do today? Fight to the death?"

"Oh, I don't think so—not yet anyway," Olivia replied. "It's only day two. Got to save some of the fun for later."

Melody chuckled. "A little dark humor goes a long way with me, Olivia. I like your style. I'm hoping whatever it is, I can be more useful today."

"You did great yesterday."

"It was you and Rose who got us through it. That's not me being modest; that's the truth. I guess riddles aren't my strong point. But if it comes to anything physical, I assure you I can pull my weight. I want to contribute. I don't want to just get through this through other people's hard work."

Olivia put a hand on Melody's back. "I assure you, the only thing I care about is getting away from here with all of our lives still intact. It's not about who *pulls their weight.*"

"Isn't life always about that though?" Melody asked, her eyes pained. "If you're not useful… you disappear. And if you can't keep up with the pack… you just get left behind."

Olivia understood now what she was afraid of. The first task had been a team effort. If they were split up, would the outcome be different? If some of them died, would the ones left behind be less likely to survive? Nothing was certain any longer.

Her thoughts were disturbed by Rose and Harry emerging from the other tent. Tess was still inside, snoring softly. Olivia offered her seat up to Rose, who took it gratefully. She looked more than a little disheveled, her cheeks flushed with color.

"Did you sleep all right?" Melody asked, rubbing Rose's back. She closed her eyes.

"The baby was kicking all night. I think my baby knows there's something going on," Rose said. "I'm… I'm worried. About the tasks. I thought I could keep up… but maybe I can't. Not if it's something physical today…"

"Don't worry about that," Olivia assured her. "Let's wait and see what the task is. If it's something the rest of us can handle alone, then you can stay at camp."

"Wait no longer, dear Ms. Knight," the Gamemaster's voice boomed across the camp. "Now that you're nearly all up, we may begin the day's festivities!"

"Oh, great," Olivia grumbled.

"I've got something wonderful in store for you today. The more observant among you have realized that there's a member of the team missing… and I'm not talking about Clive or David. No, there's another… Yara Montague, famed actress and alcoholic, is missing from your ranks. But where could she be? Shall we play a little game of Find Yara? How about this? I'll give you twelve hours to find where she is. And if you don't… well. Yara won't survive the day. That's a promise."

Brock emerged from the tent just then, his face twisted in fury. The Gamemaster chuckled knowingly.

"Oh dear, Brock. Have I riled you up? I bet you'd just love to hunt me down. But I am not the target in this game of hide and seek. The rules are simple. Find Yara, and she'll live. Find Yara, and you won't have anything to worry about. I'd say that's a good deal. But beware. Your time is about to start. And I think you'll have a hard time finding her…"

Brock was already rushing to collect his backpack, slipping on his shoes from next to the campfire they'd built for themselves.

"I'm going out there to find her," Brock said firmly. "I want a search party to join me. Who is up for it?"

"I'm with you," Olivia said immediately. Melody stood up, too, brushing herself off.

"Count me in."

"I don't want anyone coming who will slow us down," Brock said firmly, looking in Rose's direction. "No offense."

She nodded solemnly. "None taken. I'll stay... it's for the best..."

"Everyone else who is able is coming. Harry, get Henry and Tess up. I want to leave camp in five minutes so we can begin looking for Yara."

When Henry emerged from the tent, it was with a difficult limp. "These prosthetics are killing me," he said. "You go on without me. I'll stay back with Rose and protect the camp. I would only slow you down."

There was no time to disagree.

"We're coming," Elodie panted as she and Clementine came running from the woods. They were carrying more wood for the fire, but they looked ready to go. "We're well equipped for a hike. You can rely on us."

"We'll find your friend—I swear it. We want to make it up to you for leaving the group," Clementine said gently, but Brock wasn't listening any longer. Olivia knew that in his state, no one would get through to him. A person he loved had been threatened. He wouldn't stop for a single second until she was found.

They all set off at a speedy pace. Olivia knew it wasn't wise to keep up such a punishing speed, but she also knew Brock wouldn't listen to reason. The woods were clammy, and the air they breathed didn't seem to be enough. Olivia knew that of all of them, she and Brock were definitely among some of the fittest, and yet she still felt like not enough oxygen was getting into her lungs. They pushed through the jungle, swatting the foliage left and right and sloshing through the mud, but Brock was practically on a war path.

"Yara!" he shouted every few minutes. "Yara!"

As they traipsed around looking for Yara, sweat trickled unpleasantly down Olivia's spine. She had a million worries on her mind: how quickly they were getting through their supply of water; how a lot of the group were more of a hindrance than a help; but mostly, she worried about where Yara could possibly be. She called out her name until her throat was hoarse, but she heard no reply. She hoped that it would only be a matter of time before they came across her, but nothing was ever simple on the island.

Hours ticked by. They stopped several times, but never for more than a few minutes. Brock drove them forward, determined, rushing through the undergrowth—and then suddenly tumbled to the ground.

"Brock!" Olivia shouted, rushing forward, but he was already on his way back up.

"I'm fine. Don't worry about... *agh*," he groaned.

Olivia looked down, horrified to see a massive bruise already swelling up on his right ankle. "You're hurt."

"It's a sprain," he grunted, trying to put weight back on it. "Don't worry about it."

"This is not the time to be macho, Brock. What if you're seriously injured?"

He took a breath and finally looked down. Sure enough, his ankle was already swelling. "Trust me, I've broken my ankle before. It's a sprain. Just give me... give me a minute."

Olivia kneeled down and ripped a strip of fabric off his shirt, then tied it in a makeshift bandage around his foot. He didn't complain, but when she tried to lift him back up to his feet, he buckled again.

"Here," came Elodie's voice. She held out a large, straight stick, at least four feet long and a few inches in diameter. "You will need it."

"Thanks, Elodie," Brock muttered as he took it and struggled back to his feet. "When we get out of here, I'll buy ten copies of your album."

Elodie laughed bitterly. "When we get out of here, I'll give you backstage passes."

"Deal."

Once Olivia was satisfied that Brock wasn't too seriously injured, they set off once more. The hottest part of the day came and went, leaving the group even more exhausted than before. By the time they were closing in on two hours left, they had made their way all the way from one side to the other and back again, but they hadn't found a single thing.

"Maybe we're missing something," Melody wheezed.

"Like what?" asked Clementine.

"Um. I don't know. We didn't check under the dirt for trapdoors."

"Seriously?"

"Who knows what crazy things the Gamemaster set up before we got here?" Melody pointed out. "There could be traps we didn't see, signs we missed…"

"We have to keep going. To the beaches, to wherever is left," Brock insisted, putting most of his weight on the stick. He looked a little feral with his hair plastered to his head, his shirt off, and his cheeks ruddy. "I'm not giving up."

"None of us are," Melody said gently. "We'll find her if she's here."

"This is ridiculous!" Tess cried out. "She's not here! It's clearly a trick! You've run us ragged all day for nothing. I'm going back to camp."

"Fine," Brock said dismissively. "You'll only slow us down."

Olivia shot a glare at Brock. He wasn't being helpful, and she knew it was best if they stayed together.

"Tess, we shouldn't go off on our own," Olivia tried to reason, but Tess was already tearing through the trees.

"Shut up, FBI! I've had it with you! I should have gone off alone when I had the chance. You're all—"

Tess's words were cut short by her piercing scream. Olivia's heart leaped in her chest as she ran to Tess's aid, wondering what the hell had happened in the few seconds she'd been left to her own devices. But it soon became evident what had happened.

A snake had sunk its fangs deep into Tess's leg. She fell down, writhing in agony. Melody, thinking fast, ran forward with her knife raised, and plunged it into the body of the snake. It hissed and tried to bite her, but she leaped back just in time. The snake wriggled in distress, blood pouring from its body until it lay limp, but its fangs remained deep inside Tess's leg.

And Tess didn't stop screaming. Her eyes were wide, and her face was contorted in fear and pain. The wound didn't look too bad, though it was deep, and as Olivia kneeled to look at the dead snake, her heart dropped.

"*Ophiophagus hannah*," crowed the voice of the Gamemaster overhead. "The King Cobra. One of the deadliest snakes in the world."

"You—you bastard!" Tess yelled to the sky, then groaned again in pain. Already the venom was beginning to take hold. Her leg was turning a funny shade of purple, her face was swelling up, and she was beginning to shake.

The dead viper's poison would claim her life. Of that Olivia had no doubt. She was no expert on snakes, but she had been warned about cobras, and Tess's allergies were already causing her leg to turn a funny shade of purple.

"Typical bite victims die in thirty minutes or less," the Gamemaster went on. "Oh, it would sure be a shame if you didn't have the antivenom handy."

Olivia fumbled in her pack for the first aid kit they'd been given in the supplies. She searched it frantically, hoping for some kind of antidote, but she knew in her heart that it was over for Tess.

"Damn it!" she yelled, throwing the kit on the ground. "I can't find it!"

Brock rushed in alongside her as best as he could and picked it up, rooting through it frantically. "Didn't we have some? I thought we did an inventory—"

"Well, I can't find it, Brock!"

She didn't want to lose her composure, not now, but what could she do? When a woman was dying before her and she had no way to save her?

"It's not in here," he finally said. "It must… it must have been in the other kit that David took."

FATAL GAMES

Everyone looked around as the reality of their situation set in. Maybe David had been a saboteur after all. Or maybe it had just been luck and he'd taken the pack that had the antidote. In either case, it didn't matter. Tess was going to die, and nobody could do anything about it.

Tess managed a cough through her rapidly worsening condition. "Figures. What a way to go out. Bit in the leg and stabbed in the back."

"I'm so sorry, Tess," Olivia said. She wiped away a tear from her face.

"Don't you go soft on me now, FBI," Tess groaned. She winced and seized up again. Her breathing was heavy, and every word was slow. Weak. She didn't have much time. "Just do me one favor: kill this bastard and get the hell out of here."

"I'll—I'll do that," Olivia said. "I promise."

She held the woman as she gasped for air, her skin paling with every second that passed. Melody was covering her mouth in shock, unable to believe what she was seeing before her. All Olivia could do was hold Tess until her body was still.

There was silence around the group as they all took in what had happened to Tess. How had their number dwindled so quickly again? This time it had been an accident—something that could've happened to any of them. But that didn't make it any easier to deal with.

"She… she cannot be gone," Elodie whispered. "Do something!"

"I can't. She's gone," Olivia whispered. Silence followed again. Brock wiped sweat from his brow.

"All the more reason why we have to keep going," Brock said firmly. Harry stared at him in shock.

"Have you completely lost it? A person has just died!" Elodie shrieked.

"But he is right," Clementine said, nodding to Brock. "There is another life at stake. We can't lose anyone else. We should keep going, or all of this will have been for nothing. Yara might still be alive."

"So, what? We just leave her here?" Elodie asked, her lip trembling. "It's wrong… she can't just be left alone. It feels wrong to just leave her here…"

"Stay with her," Olivia said, making a quick decision. They didn't have time to fight over the matter. She needed to be the one to take control and keep the party moving. Yara was out there waiting for them, and the few minutes they had remaining were slipping through their fingers. If Elodie wanted to stay, it would be one less person to worry about. "The rest of us will keep going. Yara might still be able to be saved. But you can make sure Tess goes in peace."

Elodie nodded, her lip trembling as she kneeled beside Tess's still body. Melody handed her knife to her, giving Elodie a pointed look.

"In case there's more trouble," Melody said. Elodie nodded, cradling the knife to her chest like it was a child. Olivia didn't want to leave her there. If there were more snakes around, Elodie wouldn't stand a chance. But thinking of Yara alone and scared and even more vulnerable than the rest of them made her want to push forward. Elodie had made her choice. Now Olivia had to make hers.

The rest of them carried on. They had to. They had to make their expedition worth it. Brock led the way again, thrashing through the thicker trees to get down to the beach. Time was running out for them. They had to make every second count. Olivia didn't even have a watch to tell her how long they had left to find Yara, but she knew it wasn't long. For all they knew, they had had only seconds to spare. Or they were already too late.

They made it to the beach as planned. Brock was shambling along the shoreline now, looking for anything out of the ordinary. Olivia and the others kept up as best as they could, sweeping the sands for any sign of life. Since Melody had mentioned traps, Olivia kept her eyes on her feet, scared of what they might come across.

They kept on searching, but time was escaping them faster and faster. The sun would be going down soon. Olivia knew that if they didn't make it to Yara by then, she would die, and the whole thing would be for nothing.

"Look! Out there!" Clementine cried out, pointing across the waters. In the distance, there was a jagged rock being whipped by the vicious sea.

And atop it, there sat a woman.

"Oh my God," Brock said, his jaw dropping. "Yara…"

CHAPTER SEVENTEEN

Olivia immediately knew what she had to do. Yara was out there, scared and alone. If she felt capable of swimming to shore, she would've done it by now. Someone was going to have to swim out there and rescue her.

And she knew it had to be her.

Brock wasn't strong enough to make the swim. Yara was scared, and she might not trust someone she didn't know.

Olivia was going in after her.

She began to take off her boots, not wanting anything weighing her down. She considered taking off her jacket, too, but the waters were icy cold. She didn't want to freeze out there. Brock looked at her, panic-stricken.

"Olivia, no… you can't."

"You're hurt. And you're not a good enough swimmer. You'll both drown out there," Olivia said bluntly. Brock shook his head.

"No. The water is too choppy. No one should go out there. And you're already exhausted…"

"Brock, if I don't go, she'll die. No one else here is going to go out there for a woman they've never met before. This is our only chance."

"I can't let you do it."

"Brock, listen to me. We're running out of time. If you don't let me go now, it'll be even more dangerous. Those waves aren't going to slow down, and God knows how long Yara has been out there. Let me do this before it's too late. You don't want her to die, do you?"

"Of course not, but I don't want to lose you too!"

"You won't," Olivia said forcefully. "You have to trust me. I can do this. I *will* do this."

Brock wavered before taking a step back. After hesitating a moment, she reconsidered and took her jacket off. She knew from her swim a few days before that it would only make her heavier, and the swim would soon warm her up. She was going to need all the strength she could muster if she was going to get Yara back to shore in one piece.

She winced as she waded out into the water. It was cold despite the warmth of the day, but there was no time to get used to it. She dove forward, windmilling her arms against the harsh tides. It was going to be a hard swim, and it would be worse on the way back bringing Yara along with her. But at least then she'd be swimming with the tide. It was exhausting work, and salt water splashed in her eyes and ears. Olivia had to keep telling herself that she wasn't drowning, that she was making progress. She couldn't see much, but she hoped she was swimming in the right direction.

"Olivia! I'm over here. Please, help me."

Olivia followed the sound of Yara's desperate pleas. She hadn't been in the water more than a few minutes, but she could feel her muscles aching. She still hadn't fully recovered from the swim two days before. But she told herself she could rest once she had Yara safely back to shore. The thought of what might happen to both of them if she stopped kept her going. Her will to survive was outweighing her fears and physical limitations.

She could hear muffled cries of encouragement from the shore even as water filled her ears. The cheers of the others gave her a dose of hope. She spluttered as she kept swimming, but as her head bobbed above the water, she caught a glimpse of Yara close by, shivering on the rock. Olivia only hoped that Yara would be able to help at least a little as they swam back, or it was going to be close to impossible.

Olivia reached out for the rock, needing something to hold on to. But then a big wave caught her off guard, slamming her body into the side of the rock. She gasped in pain as her head smacked the jagged edge of the rock and Yara screamed somewhere above her as Olivia's dizziness allowed her to be swept up by the waves again. The world was spinning a little, and the violent waves made her feel like she was on a broken rollercoaster. She grappled for something to hold on to, but all her hands found were the deep expanse of water and empty space.

Then she was under. The water swallowed her whole. Her eyes opened, and all she could see was a greenish blue haze around her. She wondered if this was the last thing she'd see. It felt like her body was heavier than before… that it might pull her under even more…

Then she felt something grab onto her shirt and pull. Yara was hauling her out of the water. Olivia's burning lungs seized the chance to breathe once again, and she felt reborn, even if only for a moment. Olivia managed to grab on to a crevice in the rock, coughing out salt water.

"You're bleeding," Yara gasped, nodding to the side of Olivia's head. Now she could feel salt water settling inside the gash, and she understood that she'd be in deep trouble if they didn't get back to safety quickly. She didn't think the wound alone was life-threatening, but with exhaustion cramping her muscles and dizziness setting in, she didn't have much push left inside her. She swallowed back nausea, taking several deep breaths as she fixed Yara with a look.

"We can't stay here, or we'll die. Do you understand?"

Yara nodded, her face pale and desperate. Olivia gripped her arm.

"We can make it back. It's not that far. We just have to be quick, and we have to use all of our strength."

"I can't swim well."

"It doesn't matter. I'll support you as much as I can. You can hold on to me, but I need you to kick your legs and propel with your arm as much as you can. If you don't, we'll both drown. I'm not going to sugarcoat it. We have to work together. Got it?"

Yara steeled herself with a breath and blinked away her tears.

Olivia took her hand. "Okay. Let's go."

"Are you sure? Right now?"

"We don't have time to recover. The water is getting wilder," Olivia said, tugging Yara's arm. "Slide into the water. I've got you."

Olivia fought off the urge to be sick as she and Yara plunged back into the water. She kept an iron grip on Yara's arm until she'd adjusted to the icy water. Then, she began the grueling swim back to shore, pulling Yara along as best as she could. It made everything ten times harder, and it was hard to keep a grip on her arm as she used the other to swim, but she refused to let go. She wasn't going back without her. She'd never forgive herself if Yara died because of her. Both of them would make it back.

Or neither of them would.

She could hear her team calling out to her again, guiding them back to the safety of the shore. Olivia could feel a pulsing in the side of her head as blood poured from her wound, but she suspected it wasn't as bad as it felt. Once she was back on dry land, she would assess the damage. Brock had a first aid kit.

But she had to survive that long first.

The last few hundred yards felt harder than the entire swim. Her body was cramping up, her lungs gasping for air, her numb hands losing their grip on Yara. But she crawled onward, determined. *The Gamemaster can't win. The Gamemaster can't win. The Gamemaster can't win…*

But maybe he would. A wave smacked her in the face, and then another, and Olivia found herself weakening. She came up for breath just as another came over her and then her burden suddenly felt light. She fought back to the surface to find that Yara had been pushed away from her, and now, the two were rapidly drifting apart even as Yara desperately struggled back to her.

"No!"

It was not her voice that said that. Nor was it Yara's. She couldn't quite process it until a pair of strong hands grasped her.

"Come on!" said Brock.

It was the boost she needed. Brock wasn't the strongest swimmer in the world, and by the way he was straining and grunting on his injured ankle, he was clearly in a lot of pain. But it would be enough for the final push. He held her on his shoulder and steered her toward Yara, where he grasped her hand, and together, all three of them kicked as hard as they could to the shore.

She only noticed they had made it when her clawing hands found some rocks and sand below. She opened her eyes and gasped out in shock as she saw that she was almost on the sand. Clementine was rushing forward to help her and Yara, followed by Melody. She let out a stifled sob as they pulled her onto the beach, and she was finally able to lie down and gasp for air.

She had defied death once again.

CHAPTER EIGHTEEN

OLIVIA GREEDILY SUCKED AS MUCH AIR AS SHE COULD into her burning lungs as Yara collapsed onto the sand, spluttering and sobbing. Olivia wanted to scream at the Gamemaster for what they were doing to them all. Poor Yara had grown even paler than she had been the last time Olivia saw her, and she had purple circles under her eyes. She could easily have died out there on that rock. But wasn't that what the Gamemaster had hoped? That the waves would take them both? The Gamemaster wasn't rooting for them to win.

Not when their deaths would be so hard-hitting back home.

Though her head throbbed and she was a little worse for wear, Yara was in a worse position. Olivia quickly turned her attention to Yara, pushing her onto her side and patting her back, getting her to cough up the sea water that had entered her mouth. Yara retched, and Olivia felt terrible, but she knew Yara needed to get it out of her system.

The others stood around them in an almost protective circle. Olivia wondered if the millions watching the livestream were enjoying the show. She clenched her fists, angry with the world. But she was more than glad to see that Yara had made it through the ordeal. And now they'd completed another task safely. Or as safely as possible.

She tried not to think about what it had cost them. She hadn't forgotten their fallen companion lying dead in the trees, a victim of circumstances. Olivia had to force herself to count their blessings. Two lives had been saved when they made it to the shore. That had to mean something.

"Are you okay?" Brock asked gently, bending down beside the two women. Olivia wasn't sure which of them he was talking to, but she said nothing, looking at Yara for answers. She sounded like she could barely breathe, but she nodded nonetheless. Brock laid a kiss on Yara's salty forehead, then one on Olivia's lips. The relief on his face said it all. He was worried they wouldn't make it back. Once again, Olivia had put Brock through hell. She was beginning to understand why he was so eager to abandon their working together. When they were together, it seemed like everyone out there was determined to pull them apart.

"Here," Melody said, passing Brock an antiseptic wipe from the first aid kit. "Clean the wound off. Then we can put a bandage over it to stop the bleeding."

Olivia had almost forgotten her own wound until Brock pressed the wipe to her bloodied face. It stung badly, but even as she winced, she knew there was no way around it. She gritted her teeth and allowed Brock to clean the wound before patching her up gently. He pressed a kiss over the wound, and Olivia smiled a little. She felt completely miserable, but the sweetness of the gesture was enough to keep her going.

"Let's get them back to camp," Brock said decisively, scooping Yara's frail body into his arms. "And then we can see about regrouping for tomorrow's tasks. Can somebody help Olivia up?"

"I'm okay," Olivia insisted, rising up on her knees and then to her feet. She felt a little unsteady, but she said nothing.

Everyone set to their tasks solemnly. The day had been like a constant heart attack—terrifying and heart-wrenching. Though Olivia insisted she was fine, Melody wrapped an arm around Olivia's waist and helped her along the beach. She felt a little better now that they were out of the water, but the throbbing in her head hadn't subsided. She suspected it would continue for a while, but it was a reminder of the fact that they'd survived. That was something to hold on to.

They all made their way back along the beach, avoiding the wooded area where Tess had died. Back at camp, Rose stood in terror upon their approach, like she didn't know what was coming toward her. She placed her hand over her heart, relieved that they'd returned.

"Is everyone okay?"

Olivia and Brock exchanged a look. That was a question neither of them could answer out loud. So much had happened since they went in search of Yara. They might have her now, but Tess's body was still out there in the woods, and who knew what had become of Elodie. Olivia was exhausted from the swim and had no idea how to put her thoughts into words. So instead, she sat down and allowed Henry to check her over entirely, catching her breath slowly. That was more than enough to focus on.

"Tess didn't make it," Melody told Rose quietly. Rose let out a small hiccupping sound, covering her mouth in shock. Yara settled close to the fire, hugging her knees as her salty hair began to dry around her face. Everyone looked like the trauma of the day was catching up to them.

Everyone gathered around the fire, and Elodie soon returned, too, from the woods. She swallowed tearfully.

"Someone came… someone came and took Tess away," she whispered. No one said anything in response. It was too raw, too real. And now, Yara was coming to a little, hugging her legs and shivering by the campfire.

"What happened to you?" Brock asked her gently as he passed her some water. "You weren't on the island with us this whole time, surely?"

Yara's teeth were chattering as she shook her head. She took a sip of water and then stared off into the distance, trauma glazing her eyes over. "I don't know where I was. It's all been… a blur."

"Take your time," Olivia told her gently.

"I remember the plane going down. I… I think I hit my head as we were trying to get to the emergency exit. And then I woke up, and I was in a cave. There were all these… these cameras pointing at me. And a person in a golden mask… they spoke to me. All I could see was these piercing, blue eyes staring me down. They told me that I was going to change everything for them."

"Was it a man or a woman?"

Yara shook her head. "I… I couldn't tell you. They weren't tall… but their body was pretty covered up, and they had a voice changer. They could've been anyone."

"The Gamemaster," Henry supplied sullenly.

Yara nodded weakly. "All I know is… they want us all to suffer. That they're not just doing this for entertainment… they're doing it because it makes them happy. I get the feeling that they've been planning this for a very long time."

Olivia felt goosebumps crawling all over her skin. It wasn't news to her that the Gamemaster had a sick mind, but hearing about Yara's encounter with the creep was enough to make her feel uneasy. She was the only one of them who had been face to face with the Gamemaster, and it shocked Olivia that she had lived to tell about it.

She'd been searching her mind the whole time for motives of why they were all there, and yet she couldn't work it out. Some of them were connected—Brock, Olivia, Yara and Henry—but the rest of them, she wasn't so sure. Why would the Gamemaster target all of them like this? Were some of them just collateral damage? Or could this have happened to anyone?

Yara continued to shiver, even as she moved closer to the heat of the fire.

"Here, let's get you covered up," Brock said, but Yara shrugged him off.

"No, no... I'm okay," she said, though beads of sweat were gathering on her forehead. She hugged her knees even closer. "It's the alcohol withdrawal. It's making me sick. There's nothing you can do. I just have to get through it. I'm feeling hot and cold all the time."

Olivia gently took Yara's wrist and felt her pulse. She was no expert, but she could tell it wasn't at a normal rate, thudding hard against the pad of her thumb. Olivia was worried that the shock of the cold water they'd swam in wouldn't help either. She knew basic first aid, but she didn't think there was much they could do for Yara at that stage, apart from just keep her strength up. She rubbed Yara's back, worried that she might drop dead at any second. It was no joke what Yara was putting her body through, and if she didn't make it, it would destroy any hope Olivia and Brock had left.

"Have you eaten?"

Yara shook her head. Melody, who had been watching the interaction, reached inside her pocket and brought out a protein bar, passing it into Yara's trembling hands.

"Here," she said gently. "This might help a little. Speaking from experience."

Olivia felt a tug at her heart. Melody was so young. It pained her to know that she had been through the same struggles as Yara already, atop everything else she'd already mentioned. Olivia reminded herself that you never truly know people's struggles unless they tell you. But there was kindness in Melody's gaze as she offered her food to a stranger. It was good to see, at least, that they hadn't all lost their humanity, despite their circumstances.

"Thank you," Yara whispered, taking the protein bar. She could barely open it with her shaking hands, but she managed it eventually, taking a tentative bite. Brock caught Olivia's eye and nodded toward the woods, clearly wanting a chance to talk alone. Olivia nodded in return.

"We'll be back in just a minute," Olivia said to Yara before heading away from the group with Brock. She could see the pain and exhaustion on his face. After the day they'd had, it was no surprise. When they were far enough away, he turned to her and took her hand.

"Thank you. For what you did today. I was worried… I was worried if I tried to make the swim that neither of us would've made it back. Or else I would've gone out there myself," he murmured. She squeezed his hand.

"I would never have allowed that to happen. I'm just glad she's okay."

"Me too… but I'm worried as well."

"I understand why. You think she's not going to be able to keep up with us all when we're facing the challenges."

Brock nodded. "Not just that though. It's like she said. She's sick. This is no place for a recovering alcoholic. She's in no state to be able to survive here. And not just her… look at Rose. And look what happened to Tess. So far, we have been given team tasks, but I think that's going to change soon. If it's true that there are spies inside the group, then soon they're going to start showing themselves. It would have been almost too obvious— too easy—to think Tess and Clive were spies, just because they were jerks. I think we have to be super careful, or we're going to lose more people."

Olivia nodded solemnly. She could still see Tess's face turning red, her body writhing in pain. It had been a horrible accident, but it could've happened to any of them. It still could. There was so much to consider if they wanted to stay alive. How many variables were there that could get them all killed? Too many to count. It was as if the entire island was designed to keep them on their toes, to entertain the masses. And, well, it was.

It was only day two of seven. What else was in store for them?

"Yara is strong. I think if she has a chance to rest tonight, she might be able to contribute by the morning. But if not… we'll carry her through. We'll make sure she doesn't get hurt."

"It's a little late for that," Brock growled, his jaw clenched. "If I ever catch the person responsible for all of this…"

"I know. I know," Olivia said. "There will be hell to pay. But we can't let anger get in the way right now. We have to push through to survive. We have to be careful."

Brock nodded again. There was a look of defeat in his eyes. Olivia cupped his cheek.

"I know you don't have faith that we can get through this… but we will. I promise; we will. And now that we're all back together… nothing can take Yara away again. We'll make sure of it."

"Good," Brock said, his expression pained. "Because we almost lost her today. I don't want that all to be for nothing."

CHAPTER NINETEEN

Morning hit Olivia hard. Her muscles were aching from physical exertion after her hellish swim, and she was definitely tempted to go back to sleep for a while. There was nothing truly stopping her until the Gamemaster's ominous voice told them what they'd be doing next. But she sat up slowly, stretching her arms to the sky and glancing around her to see if anything had changed while she was asleep. Henry and Brock were asleep beside her in the tent, so she quietly exited the tent and embraced the morning air.

The camp seemed calm and quiet while her new companions slept. Olivia knew it was a good thing. They would need their rest for whatever the day might hold. None of the others had risen yet, and there was no sign of David. She had to take that as a positive for now.

Some of the group were now fully convinced that he was a saboteur. It had been another test, and they had failed, and now Tess was dead because he had stolen the antivenom in the first aid kit. Olivia had to push back on that. It could have been that he simply didn't know that there were deadly snakes on the island or that his first aid kit contained the only cure. It could have been a coincidence. Not that she put much stock in those.

The real question would be what to do if David returned and tried to win back their good graces. They'd argued in circles about it all night until they basically decided there was no point in even wasting the mental energy on it when they should be resting.

Yara must have slept, too, because she wasn't by the fire. Olivia was glad that she had been welcomed by the others, at least for now. Their new addition to the camp had changed the mood. No one really knew her outside of Brock and Olivia, which seemed to make some of them uneasy. Plus, it was obvious from the moment they found her that she was going to be a burden on the group. She wasn't fit to contribute much at all, and Olivia worried what that would mean for her. There were still five days to get through, and it wasn't about to get any easier.

Still, she wasn't turning her back on Yara. More than ever, she needed someone to look out for her.

Olivia hugged her knees close to her chest and closed her eyes for a few moments to prepare herself for whatever the day might hold. She wasn't sure how much more her body could take physically. She had been carrying the team from the start, and it was beginning to take a toll. She needed to rest up if she was going to be of any use. She hoped that the challenges they faced that day would be more mentally challenging than physically.

She felt a hand gently rest on her back and turned to see that Brock had been roused from sleep. He'd left the flap of the tent open, and Olivia could hear Henry snoring inside. They both chuckled, and Brock offered her a smile.

"Hey," she whispered. "Sleep better last night?"

"Much better," he replied. Olivia knew he could rest easier now that they'd found Yara. The war wasn't over, but they'd won one battle. They had to take each victory as it was given to them, even after everything they'd lost. Olivia's mind returned to Tess and Clive. It made her feel like they were failing at their job. They were supposed to be keeping everyone alive, not watching them get picked off one by one. If a person died for each day they were on the island, there would be five more bodies piling up. Olivia didn't want that to happen.

"It's going to be all right," Brock told her, reading her mind as he so often did. "What happened to Clive… he was being reckless. He didn't follow the rules, and he paid for it. And nature took Tess out. We didn't know there were deadly snakes here… we couldn't have predicted that would happen. But what we do have control over… we can handle. No one else has to get hurt."

Olivia's arms tightened around her legs. "Something tells me we won't have any choice in the matter. The Gamemaster wants to see blood. That's what will keep the viewers coming in. And they'll be hungry for more today. Whatever our task is… I think it's going to end badly."

"Oh, Olivia… you're much too perceptive," the Gamemaster's voice said over the speakers. Olivia gritted her teeth.

"I was beginning to think it was too quiet."

"I'm never far away, Olivia… and you're right. I'm hungry for some action today. *Starving*, in fact," the Gamemaster purred. "But I'm no monster. You'll all have a chance to save your own skins. Only one person will die today… and I guess it's up to all of you who it will be."

Olivia didn't even want to imagine what that would mean. Would they have to kill someone themselves? Olivia wasn't going to allow that to happen. The others might be willing to do the Gamemaster's bidding to save their own skins, but Olivia drew the line at them turning on one another. As if things weren't bad enough.

The others were beginning to wake from their sleep. The twins were wide-eyed and afraid as they left their tent, clutching one another's hands. Melody and Harry exchanged an uncomfortable look in the mouth of their tent, and Rose cradled her stomach maternally as she joined Olivia at the fire. Yara crawled out of her tent just to lay on the ground, staring into space like she couldn't process what she was hearing. She looked even weaker than she had the day before.

"Your task is simple. I know you all know how to play hide and seek. But have you ever played for your life before?" the Gamemaster asked. "In one hour, a trained assassin is going to arrive on the island. By then, you will all have picked a hiding spot… I hope. The assassin will hunt you all down until they find one of you. That person will have a choice—kill or be killed. But given that my assassin is highly trained, I'm sure we know who is going to win that fight."

Olivia felt her face harden. There was absolutely no chance she was allowing an assassin to kill her, or any of her friends. Her hands turned into fists. If it came to it, she wouldn't hesitate to do what she had to do protect her new comrades.

She looked over at Brock, who gave her a determined nod. He may not have been a good swimmer, but he was a hell of a fighter. Without even a discussion, she knew he would throw his life on the line to protect them, too, just as she would.

"The assassin will be given twelve hours to find one of you. After that time, if you're all still alive, then you win. The game will be over the second we lose a participant. The game should be fair, after all. It would be a little boring if you all died before the end of the day, don't you agree?"

Olivia wanted to scream at the Gamemaster. To grab them by the throat and make them suffer the way they were all suffering on the island. She couldn't bear the thought of any of the people gathered with them dying that day.

"So, it goes without saying, you should all start looking for a good place to hide," the Gamemaster said wolfishly. "But be warned. You can run, but you can't hide. My assassin is the best in the game. Don't think you'll slip away so easily. Wherever you go, they will be one step behind you… so don't hesitate. Get out while you still can."

The static of the speaker concluded the Gamemaster's speech. Olivia turned to the terrified faces of the group. They needed someone to give them comfort before they all spiraled.

"Don't listen to what the Gamemaster is saying. This island is huge. There must be places we can hide away without being found. But we should really get moving. We don't have much of a head start."

"You heard what they said. There's going to be a… a trained assassin coming for us all. We can't just BS our way through this one," Harry said, his youthful face creased with concern. He folded his arms around himself. "And we can't stick together."

"Why not?" Elodie asked, chewing her lip. "If we stay with Olivia, Brock and Henry, they may be able to protect us."

"No," Yara said, shaking her head. Her face seemed even paler than the day before. "We all have to split up. What happens if the assassin finds us all clumped together? They might try to kill us all. The rules weren't clear about what would happen if the assassin found a group… just that they'd have to kill or be killed."

"Yeah, so if there's a group of us, surely we can take down one assassin?" Harry replied.

"Maybe, or maybe not. But we might also be shot down before we can stop it. And if we don't spread out, we'll be easier to find. It would be like waving a flag over our heads saying, 'Here I am!'"

"Yara… you can't be considering going off alone," Brock said, shaking his head. "We only just got you back. And you're… you're not well."

"I'm well enough to curl up and hide someplace for a while. It doesn't sound too strenuous to me. In fact, I think that's maybe what I'd like to do most today," she said, rolling her eyes. Then she sighed, looking guilty as she reached to pat Brock's arm. "I know you think you can protect us all. I know you're trying to do the right thing. But Harry's right. It's more dangerous if we stay in one place together."

"Olivia and I came here to try to protect you all," Brock said. "And you might feel comfortable going off on your own, but I don't think it's a good idea. Not for anyone. We won't have any control if we're separated. And while some of us have some training, let's be honest—most of you wouldn't stand a chance. Is that a risk you're really willing to take?"

Olivia didn't know how to feel about it. On one hand, clumping together would certainly make them easier targets. But if Olivia and Brock had an opportunity to take the assassin down, for the sake of the innocent people on the island, then wasn't it worth trying? That was why they'd agreed to go to the island in the first place—to save lives. And looking around her, she already had concerns about some of them not surviving the day. Melody and Harry seemed capable of looking after themselves, as did Elodie and Clementine, since they had one another's back. But to defend against an elite assassin? Would the killer have weapons? Guns? In any situation, she just couldn't see how the civilians would manage.

And that wasn't even to mention Rose and Yara. Neither were in any fit state to look after themselves, and even Henry was struggling on his new prosthetics, which would slow him down in a chase. It seemed risky leaving them to their own devices if they all wanted to survive the day.

On one hand, they had a chance to all make it out alive.

But on another, more than one of them might die if they weren't careful.

"I… I don't want to be alone," Rose said, her lip wobbling. "I don't feel safe."

"Well, we're not safe," Melody said bluntly. "This island is designed to kill us. It's not going to be easy. But you'll be fine, Rose. No one is going to kill a pregnant woman, even if they find you first. You'll be okay, I promise. The rest of us? It's fair game." She stood up and brushed herself off, grabbing a protein bar from their stockpile. "I'm not wasting any more time. I'm going to find somewhere to hide, and I'm not moving until it's all over, one way or another. I guess I'll see you all on the other side… I'll come back to this spot at nightfall. I hope you all make it."

Melody stalked off, leaving everyone else in the camp silent. Olivia was shocked that Melody had been so callous about the situation, but she could also see how survival instincts were starting to kick in. Everyone was in fight or flight mode, and it was making them think more about covering their own backs than anyone else's. Elodie and Clementine exchanged a look with one another before standing too.

"We will take our chances together," Clementine said with a decisive nod. She threaded her fingers through Elodie's. "Good luck to you all. I… I hope we will see you tonight."

The pair of them walked off into the wilderness together, taking some supplies on their way out. Olivia walked over to Rose and put her hands on her shoulders.

"It's going to be okay. But maybe Yara is right. We might be safest alone," Olivia said gently. She didn't want to leave Rose, or any of the others, but there was sense in what Yara was saying. The Gamemaster had really thought about how to tear them all apart, clearly. She had a distinct feeling that the Gamemaster was trying to split them up, to make them feel vulnerable on their own, and it was working. But she had faith that most of them could protect themselves. It was only twelve hours to get through. They could do it.

"What do I do? I don't know how to survive this," Rose said tearfully. Olivia pointed to the woods.

"Walk for as far as you can manage. Try to find somewhere concealed. At the first sign of trouble, make sure you lay low. Don't move, even if you're scared. You're more likely to give yourself away. You'll be okay."

Rose nodded, looking terrified. Olivia wished she had something better to offer to her, but they were all in the same boat. There was nothing they could do except play by the rules and hope to make it out alive. Olivia pressed a bottle of water and several food items into Rose's hands and sent her on her way gently. It was hard to watch her walking away—harder than watching the others do the same. She had two lives to think about. Olivia swallowed and hoped that Melody was right about Rose's safety. That had to be some small blessing to hold on to.

She knew she had to think about finding her own hiding spot, but there were still others at the camp. Henry was getting to his feet unsteadily, and Olivia's heart squeezed at the thought of something happening to him. He would be slowed down by his prosthetics, and Olivia wondered if she should take a chance and go with him. At least together they should be capable of taking down a killer. But as though he knew what she was thinking, he caught her eye and shook his head.

"I can take care of myself," he insisted. "I've survived worse, right? I can take Yara, too, if you think it's a good idea?"

"I'll be fine," Yara snapped. Then she rubbed at her sweating forehead, looking ashamed at her outburst. "Sorry. I'm just… I'm just tense. I can do this. Don't worry about me. I'm going to find somewhere to stick it out alone."

Before anyone else could argue, she was heading off alone, her legs seeming to tremble as she walked off. And then all of a sudden, it was just Olivia and Brock, standing opposite one another by the burned-out campfire. Olivia took his hand.

"I don't want to leave you."

"I don't want to leave you either. But we should split. You know it makes sense," Brock said. "Besides… I know you're making it out, no matter what. No one is a match for you. If someone is going to wind up dead, it certainly won't be you. They would be stupid to try and mess with you."

Olivia didn't want to cry. She couldn't. Not now.

He pressed a kiss to her lips, and Olivia wished she could cling to him just a little longer and make the moment last. She couldn't bear the thought that she would never see him alive again. But before she could tell him just how much she cared, he was pulling away. He grabbed a few supplies and set off as quickly as he could on his weak ankle, leaving Olivia alone.

Her heart hardened. Now that it was just her, she could focus on getting out of there. She knew she had what it took to survive the day. She picked up a knife from their cooking supplies. She wasn't taking any chances. Then she grabbed some food and water before heading off into the trees.

Her hammering heart kept her moving. She had no idea how much time she had lost already, but the sooner she found somewhere to hunker down, the safer she'd feel. As she jogged through the forest, she caught glimpses of the others meandering through the trees, looking for hiding spots of their own. She felt sick at the nostalgia it gave her of playing hide and seek in her childhood. She'd never look back on those memories fondly again, that was for sure. It wasn't so fun when it was a game of survival.

She pushed farther on, wanting to put as much distance between her and the other contestants as possible. Whatever happened that day, she didn't want to hear what went on, and she certainly didn't want anyone to hear her fight for her life if it came to that. She hoped to find somewhere, anywhere, that she would be truly alone.

Time was ticking, and she could feel it escaping her. She could see nothing but trees. Perhaps hiding was going to be harder than she imagined. She didn't like the idea of being out in the open, running through the trees all day to evade a killer. There had to be somewhere better she could go. She just had to keep looking.

But her trek was taking it out of her, and she knew she was close to running out of time. She wondered if the assassin was already on the island, just waiting for their opportunity to pounce. It made her feel sick. She felt naked without the gun she usually carried when she was dealing with a situation like this. Her knife didn't feel like it was enough to protect her.

She was about to change her direction when her foot collided with something beneath the dirt, almost tripping her up. She frowned and bent down, feeling around in the muck for what it might be. Her hand grappled onto something that made her heart skip a beat. It was a handle. She pulled on it and was shocked when the earth moved and a wooden latch lifted up.

She'd found a trap door.

CHAPTER TWENTY

OLIVIA STARED DOWN THROUGH THE TRAP DOOR, HER heart pounding. It was too dark to see much of what was down there, but curiosity was already getting the better of her. Knowing the Gamemaster and their antics, it was entirely possible that the bunker was a trap. Perhaps the assassin was waiting down there for her in the dark, or maybe it was booby trapped. But Olivia knew that her time was running out and she needed somewhere to hide before the assassin got to her first. It would be embarrassing to die out in the open just because she was too scared to take a risk. She decided she would rather take her chances in the dark bunker than out in the open.

She saw that there was a ladder leading down, so she clambered onto it, descending into the darkness. Her arm brushed a long piece of string beside the ladder, and she tugged it, wondering if it might be a light switch. Several dim lights began to fill the bunker with a warm glow and a harsh buzz. Olivia was relieved to see that nothing in the bunker looked particularly dangerous, so she decided to pull the trapdoor closed and settle down for the day.

Her heart was racing as she finally sat down on a chair in the corner for a while to catch her breath. The room was musty and muggy, but at least it was out of sight and out of mind.

She put her head in her hands and tried to deal with the reality of their situation. It was agony, wondering where her friends might be and knowing she could do nothing to help them. She knew she didn't really need to worry about Brock, and she was sure Henry could still handle himself, but Yara was in no fit state to keep herself safe, really. Then she thought of her new friends—Melody and Rose and Harry and the twins. She closed her eyes. She didn't want any of them to die. If they could just make it through the next twelve hours, everything would be okay. They could take matters back into their own hands. But if the assassin was any bit as good as the Gamemaster claimed, Olivia was sure that the day would end in tragedy.

She felt useless. She wished she had at least gone with one of the more vulnerable members of the group. She could've been there to protect Yara, or Rose. Rose certainly would've appreciated the company. But instead, Olivia was hiding alone in a bunker, unable to do anything for the next twelve hours. She cursed herself for being swept up in the moment and going along with the plan the others had concocted. It was making her feel like she'd lost control—something she hated even in the best of times.

She knew she'd go mad if she didn't give herself something to do. She looked around, taking in more of the space that she'd locked herself into. Her nose tickled with dust. Clearly, no one came down here very often, but everything was still neat and in order. She was surprised to note that it was almost like an office—there was a desk with several manila folders stacked upon it, and there was a filing cabinet against the wall. There was a giant wooden chest on the other side of the room too; Olivia stood to go take a look at it. There was no lock on it, and it opened easily. Olivia gasped when she saw that it was full of pantry foods. There were endless cans and boxes full of non-perishables. Olivia wondered what the purpose of the place was. Was it some kind of survivalist bunker? And if so, why was it there? Was someone actually spending extended amounts of time on the island?

A thin tendril of fear went down her back. Or what if it was one of the Gamemaster's hideouts?

She pushed that thought out of her mind. For better or worse, she was here now, so for the time being, she might as well make herself at home. She grabbed a can of peaches from inside the box and ate some as she investigated the rest of the bunker. She took a quick look at the desk and the folders atop it, but the folders seemed to contain stock lists of the basement. Nothing of real interest. She turned her attention to the filing cabinet, moving as quietly as she could to look inside the boxes it contained. She knew it was very unlikely that anyone would be able to hear her quietly shuffling around, but she wasn't going to take any chances. The last thing she wanted was for her nosiness to get her killed.

One of the boxes contained another pile of manila folders. She wasn't really in the mood to read, but it was better than sitting and twiddling her thumbs. She scooped all of the folders out to put on the desk, but there was something else rattling at the bottom of the box. She frowned as she went to investigate what it was. Her heart dropped when she realized…

It was a loaded gun.

Olivia wondered what the hell it was doing there. It was almost as if it had been hidden deliberately under the folders so that it wasn't in plain sight. Which meant that someone put it there deliberately for someone else… or for themselves. Olivia's heart skipped a beat. Had it been planted there for one of the Gamemaster's spies to use? Did the traitors among them know exactly where this bunker was? And if so, did that put her in danger?

It made some sense. Olivia still couldn't understand why the bunker was there in the first place. In her mind, the island was abandoned, used only for the sake of the sick games they were being put through. But now she had to question how deep this operation ran. How long had the Gamemaster been planning this endeavor? Were they the first victims to fall on the island, or had there been test runs before they arrived? She knew the Gamemaster's reign over the internet had been going on for quite a while, but nothing like this had ever come up before. She was certain she'd know about it if it had.

But that didn't mean something more secretive hadn't happened before.

Olivia sat down on the chair in the corner, turning the gun over in her hands. Was someone going to come looking for it? She certainly hoped not. If she had accidentally stumbled on the Gamemaster's base, then she was in real trouble. Still, at least she was armed now. She didn't need to worry about someone outgunning her. Besides, she'd have the element of surprise if anyone did try to get inside the basement. She held on to that thought.

She didn't think she'd be surprised if trouble came her way in the next twelve hours now. She didn't just have to worry about the assassin now. There was a possibility that the saboteurs might know the location of the bunker. The Gamemaster themselves might also be nearby. Olivia didn't want to believe that she'd put herself in a more dangerous situation than before, but it was seeming more and more likely to her now.

If she was going to figure out what was going on, she would have to investigate the bunker further. Maybe she would find something crucial there that would help her take down her enemies. If one of her group was working with the Gamemaster, then she needed to know about it. Maybe the details would be in the folders. Still gripping the gun in one hand, feeling on edge, Olivia opened the first folder. If there was something to find, she was going to hunt it down.

The first few folders didn't yield much. They were filled with more reports about the stock in the bunker. Olivia was interested to see that there were more weapons listed in the inventory, though she had no interest in hunting them down at that moment, and the file didn't specify the locations of each one. The gun would be enough to protect herself. She didn't want to be caught off guard if someone made it down into the bunker.

But the fifth folder that she stumbled across was much more interesting. When she opened it up, she saw that it contained profiles of a bunch of people Olivia had never seen before. Each profile came with a consent form and an NDA, plus a bunch of photographs of people on the island. When Olivia read closely, she realized that these weren't just ordinary people.

They were prior contestants.

Olivia singled out the first profile and flipped through it, reading through some of the information.

I, Daniel Ramirez, consent to participating in the Island Games for seven days between the 4th and 10th of April, 2020. I acknowledge that death during the Games is possible, and I declare that my loved ones will take no action against the Gamemaster in the event of my death. I also promise not to speak of the Games to anyone. I acknowledge that breaking this contract will result in immediate death.

Olivia stared at the document for a long time. She flipped the page back to Daniel's profile. Over the black and white picture of him, a red X now sliced through his face. *Well, I guess he didn't survive the Games,* Olivia thought. *Either that or he broke his contract.*

There was more. Identical documents and photos, all with the exact same verbiage. Tristan Walter. Connie Merritt. Eddie Robinson. Cheryl Forbes. Paige McGowan. All of them had signed the same documents. And all of them had red X's on their faces.

Olivia found a bunch of photographs of Daniel with his group, or him being washed up on the beach, of him crouching low to hide from trouble. Then, a final gruesome photograph of him with his throat ripped out. Olivia swallowed anxiously. Had another contestant done that to him? Was it an animal attack?

Or was it an assassin? Somehow, the second option was a more comforting thought.

There was a questionnaire attached to his profile too. She flipped through it quickly, gaining some understanding of the screening process.

Why did you decide to take part in the Games?
To win the grand prize for my family. I'll do whatever it takes to get this money to them.
Are you willing to turn on other contestants if called upon to do so?
Yes. Absolutely.
Do you have any reservations about using violence to get what you want?
None at all. I'll do whatever is necessary.

Olivia swallowed. The line of questioning was disturbing in itself. It seemed that these Games had been a little different than their own. The Gamemaster had recruited the most brutal people they could find. Criminals. Thieves. People who thought nothing of betraying the others to get ahead. As she flicked through the rest of the folder, she found that most of the contestants from the beta version of the Games were dead. Two had walked away with a share of half a million apiece. According to the profiles of the contestants, they were both still alive and continuing their lives in peace. It made Olivia shudder.

But now things were starting to make sense to her. There had been others, long before they'd been there. They, too, had been put through life-threatening trials. But why? These people had signed themselves up for it, evidently. It seems like money was involved. But how had the FBI not caught on to this? Olivia guessed that the Gamemaster had kept these Games on the down-low. Maybe they'd only been live streamed to a select few on the dark web. Whatever the scenario was, at least Olivia knew now that the Gamemaster had to be filthy rich. There was no way they were pulling it off otherwise.

Olivia continued to read through the other folders. She found another folder that had instructions on the current set of participants. She found her profile first and saw that the Gamemaster had been collecting information on her for some time. They somehow knew about all of her cases from the past few years, about her family history, about things only those closest to her knew. Olivia scanned the profile.

Strengths: intelligence, at her physical peak, FBI training.
Weaknesses: Brock Tanner, her family. Prone to self-doubt. Savior complex.

Olivia almost snorted at the assessment of her character. Maybe she did have a savior complex, but she didn't see how wanting to help people was a weakness. It was part of her job, after all. Still, it worried her that she had been profiled in such a way. Whoever was out to get her would find it a lot easier if they got their hands on Brock or her family… that was for sure.

The folder continued to instruct on how to take down Olivia and Brock. It also stated that they were the main targets. Olivia frowned. Why? Who was the Gamemaster, and why did they want them to die so badly? And weren't there easier ways to kill a person than forcing them into deadly games on a desert island?

Olivia recalled what the Gamemaster had said to them the first time they spoke. That they knew about how Brock and Olivia took down ANH. It wasn't exactly private information—the case had become a nationwide news sensation, given the scale of the destruction it caused—but now it made Olivia wonder who else would care about that. Someone who worked for ANH, perhaps?

Or even the mastermind behind it all.

Olivia thought about Yara's description of the Gamemaster. She said they were a small person. Was it possible it was a woman? Was it possible that Eve Valentine was the one who had constructed such an elaborate scheme to have them killed? It did seem like it was her style. As the head of ANH, she had been responsible for terrors beyond Olivia's imagination. She'd killed so many people in the course of her career that it made

Olivia a little sick to her stomach. She was also the kind of woman who got bored easily. Maybe she had constructed the Games as a sick kind of entertainment. And now she was back again with games designed just for her worst enemies, Olivia and Brock. She wanted to publicly humiliate them for what they'd done to her. The more Olivia thought about it, the more it made sense to her.

Olivia was about to turn the next page of the document when she heard something from above her. Her heart froze. She was certain she could hear footsteps. She stood as quietly as she could, positioning herself in the shadows, with her gun aimed at the trapdoor. She wasn't going to allow anyone to take her by surprise. But who could it be? Was it another contestant on the run? Or was it the assassin?

Olivia held her breath as the footsteps stopped short of the trap door. Then she heard it creak open, sunlight streaming in from above. She held steady, waiting for a face to appear. Whoever it was knew exactly where to find the bunker, and that meant they were more likely a foe than a friend. If it wasn't the assassin, then maybe it was a saboteur. But who?

Olivia's eyes widened as a pair of legs appeared on the ladder and the figure descended. They hadn't noticed her, and their head was obscured by a hood. When they reached the base of the ladder, Olivia swallowed, her gun ready to aim.

"Turn around. Slowly," she demanded. The figure stopped dead, reaching for something on their belt.

"Don't," Olivia warned. "I'm armed. I'll shoot if I have to."

The figure sighed. Then, slowly, they turned around. Olivia blinked in surprise when she saw who it was.

"David?"

CHAPTER TWENTY-ONE

"**D**AVID… WHAT ARE YOU DOING HERE?"
David held his hands up in the air, and Olivia stared at him in shock. She didn't have many reasons to trust the man since he had run off with their supplies, but she didn't imagine that he was working with the Gamemaster. In fact, she had been sure of that when he ran off, and she had argued as such just last night. Now she wasn't so sure. Why else would he be there if he wasn't in league with the Gamemaster?

Her first question was why? What did a man of his age stand to gain from his betrayal to a bunch of strangers? And her second question was, how had he convinced himself to go through with it? How had he come to the conclusion that it was the right decision to hurt them all?

"You're the one who isn't supposed to be here," David said, raising an eyebrow at her. He nodded to the open file on the table. "And you certainly weren't supposed to find those files. I would appreciate if you'd put those back where you found them."

"You're working with the Gamemaster."

David nudged his glasses up his nose, his face unreadable. "I am, I'm afraid. No use in hiding that any longer."

"Are you… are you the assassin?"

"Fortunately for you, I'm not. I've been given the tools to kill anyone I want… but I don't intend to use them. Not unless you force my hand. I might make life more difficult for you, running off with your supplies and all, but I'm not trying to kill you. You can lower that gun."

"I don't think so, David. You took the antivenom. Tess got bit by a snake, and *you* stole the only cure. And now she's gone. As far as I'm concerned, you have blood on your hands."

He pressed his lips in a tight line. "I didn't mean to kill anyone. I thought there was anti-venom in both kits," he finally admitted. "I'm sorry, but that wasn't my fault."

Olivia scoffed. "I can't believe you. You'll do anything to keep up the pretense of being innocent. But you turned your back on us all. You took food from our mouths."

This time the determination in David's face turned to anger. "I did you a favor, going off alone. There were much worse things I could've done. I could've killed you in your sleep, Olivia. It would've been so easy to do that when you were all being so damn trusting," he snapped. "Believe me—I thought about it. The Gamemaster was willing to reward more for that kind of behavior… but I held myself back."

"Oh, how thoughtful of you!"

"You owe the fact that you're still alive to me. So do the others."

"Not Tess."

He ignored her and doubled down. "Imagine how the team would have crumbled without you, their fearless leader. That would've been a death sentence for them all. I had to do something to disrupt you all, or my contract with the Gamemaster would be

FATAL GAMES

void. But you want to act like I'm such a villain. Grow up. Besides, none of you have gone hungry, have you?"

Olivia shook her head, still unable to understand his motives. He said that the Gamemaster had offered him something… but what? What was worth this kind of treachery? What was worth making himself into the bad guy?

"I just want to know why, David. What would drive you to be so selfish? What are you getting out of this?"

David smiled. "Things you could only imagine. The Gamemaster promised me everything I've never had."

"I presume that means money, then."

"Money. Access to healthcare. A chance to live the life I was never afforded," David said, his face solemn now. "You've got to understand—not everyone on this island is filthy rich. I might've looked the part, and I know how to play the part. It's not hard when rich people are such damn idiots. Makes them easy to replicate. I ended up on that plane because I was promised the world if I came here. The rest of them? They were just on their way to another expensive retreat while the rest of the world is starving and scrimping just to get by. How am I the bad guy here? I'm just taking what's been owed to me my entire life. And if I die here… well, I have nothing to lose, do I? I had nothing in the first place."

"That's not how it works. You can't just condemn other people because your life has been hard. You're not the only one who has had a difficult life."

"Oh, I know that. I've read your file, Olivia. I know the things you've endured while you served your country. And what thanks have you ever gotten for it, hmm? Did the FBI offer you a pay raise for your trauma? Are you getting some benefits I don't know about? Because if not, I really don't know what drives you. No one would blame you for taking more than you're getting, for taking matters in your own hands. We only get one life, you know. And when we're dead, we're dead. We'll be forgotten, and no one will remember how we lived. Unless we learn to take what the world owes us."

"At what cost, David? You're willing to let other people die so that you can spend your retirement with a bit more money?

Don't you feel guilty? Don't you feel like you owe it to yourself to do better?"

David laughed. "I left guilt behind me long ago. And I'm not going back. Why should I? You might not get it, and that's okay. You've been brainwashed by the system as much as anyone. But I want to live the days I have left knowing that I can do it in comfort. I'm not just old, Olivia. I'm dying. Cancer is going to eat me up until there's nothing left of me. And what do I have to show for my life? Fifty years of backbreaking work. Eighteen years before that living in poverty, growing up in a family that didn't love me. My wife left me twenty years ago. My kids don't speak to me, the ungrateful little brats. My life has been in ruin for the longest time. Now, I want to go out with a *bang*. And I need money to do that." David shook his head. "When I'm done here, I'm going to take a vacation to the Bahamas and never come back. I'm going to do drugs and drink until my final days. And I'm going to take the experimental treatment the Gamemaster is willing to fund for me if I do their bidding. Maybe it'll buy me some time so I don't have to die feeling like my whole life was wasted."

Olivia took a calming breath, trying to get her head around it all. "So, let me get this straight… your life has been terrible. No one stuck around for you… and so you're going to help murder a bunch of random people to make up for it?" Olivia's expression hardened. She couldn't believe what she was hearing. "Have you ever considered that *you're* the problem, David? So busy wallowing in your own misery and driving people away from you that you can't see that *you* did this to yourself? That *you're* the common denominator in all of your own issues?"

David snarled and whipped a gun off his belt, making Olivia jump slightly. "Don't make me shoot you, Olivia. You know you have a lot more to lose than I do. Poor, pathetic David has nothing to live for. That's what you and everyone else has been thinking for the longest time. Well, I've made the decision to change that. And no, I don't care what that costs anyone else. I've done my fair share of worrying about people who don't do the same for me. I'm done. And if you want to make it out of this alive, I suggest you listen to me."

"Do you really think you'll win a shootout with an FBI agent, David? I don't want to kill you. You've done bad things, but I won't shoot unless I have no other choice. We can still work this out. You can just hide out here until the end of the Games. You can go home with your life and finish it in peace. Isn't that enough?"

David scoffed. "Not nearly. If that was enough for me, I wouldn't be doing this in the first place. I've got a new life waiting for me. All I need to do is make it through a few more days here and do a few more favors for the Gamemaster."

"And you trust them?"

"I'll take my chances. It's like I said. I've got everything to gain and nothing to lose. Which makes me more dangerous than you want to admit to yourself, Olivia. It means I won't hesitate to shoot you to get what I want."

Olivia bristled with rage. He was right.

"So, here's how this is going to go down. We're both going to walk out of here when the assassin finds their victim, or when the twelve hours is up. I'm going to allow you to leave… but I'll return to the group with a message. The Gamemaster has told me to up my game, or I'll get nothing… so I'm going back to the group and telling them that *you're* the saboteur. I'll even tell them that you're the assassin for good measure."

"Are you crazy, David? No one is going to believe that. Brock and Henry and Yara… they know me. They know that's impossible. They'll sway the group. And the others trust me much more than they trust you."

"They're all going to be scared and paranoid after whatever goes down today. They won't be thinking straight. I think I can sway them. And if I can, then you're going to have a target on your back. I don't think there will be much chance of you surviving if you're isolated without any supplies… but hey, maybe you'll prove me wrong. I guess we'll find out. You're resourceful. You can make it work."

"David, don't do this. Think about what you're doing."

"I've done plenty of thinking. I'm not changing my mind," David said. His gun was trained perfectly at her, even though his hands were shaking. "You might not be able to see things from my perspective, but I'm tired of trying to make people see my side of the story. This is my life, and I'm the master of it. I won't be told what to do anymore. Especially not by the likes of you."

Olivia wished she could knock some sense into the old man. On some level, she understood why he was the way he was. He felt slighted by the world, like he was an outsider looking in on the life he could've had. But that didn't excuse his cruelty. At his core, he was a bad man, and Olivia knew it. She wasn't getting out of this one without him shooting at her or forcing her to walk away. She could end it now and kill him, but that wasn't who she was. At least out there alone, she would have a chance to live.

Olivia was jolted by the sound of a gunshot in the distance. Her heart felt hollow. She prayed that there would be some other sound, some sign that someone had survived… but there was only silence. David's mouth twisted into a smile.

"Looks like the assassin found their victim. I wonder who they found first. Maybe it was that boyfriend of yours."

Olivia felt fury rise inside her, hot and raw. "Why are you being so cruel? We haven't done anything to you, David. Why would you say something so callous? Someone could be dead. Maybe someone I care about. And you're joking about it?"

David's face flickered with brief guilt, but he soon recovered. He nodded to the ladder. "Drop the gun. It's time for you to go. I'll give you ten seconds to move, or I'll shoot."

Olivia shook her head in disbelief. She couldn't believe this was happening. But she didn't want blood to be spilled. Cruel as David was, she thought he would honor his promise. He was so on the edge that she didn't want to give him the final push. She placed the gun on the table. She wished she'd been given more time to read through the documents, to find out more about who was working for the Gamemaster, but she wouldn't make it back there again. She had to go if she wanted to live.

She walked toward the ladder and slowly climbed to freedom. The hot sun beat down on her as she opened the trapdoor. It had only taken the assassin a matter of hours to hunt one of them down. Someone was lying dead out there, but there was nothing she could do for them now. It was her turn to save herself.

She began to run. There was an assassin close by. She wasn't taking her chances, just in case the Gamemaster broke the rules and had them kill someone else. She had to find somewhere else to hide again. But she couldn't go back to camp.

She'd have to make her own way.

CHAPTER TWENTY-TWO

O LIVIA WOKE UNDERNEATH A TREE WITH A POUNDING heart and the sun beating down on her face. Her cheeks were hot, and she realized she was burning. Sitting up slowly, she assessed the damage—she was sweating, her face peeling, her head pounding. It was the first time she'd slept outside since the night on the beach without a tent to cover her up. Now, she was overheating, her body stiff from her uneasy night of rest. She knew that she had to be dehydrated, too, when she realized how dry her tongue was. After all, she was trapped on a deserted island with no water.

She realized shortly after running away from David that she didn't have any supplies to keep her going. She'd left everything she had with her there, including the water and snacks she'd taken for the day. She considered going back to the bunker to try and pilfer some of the supplies, or maybe even a weapon, but it felt too risky. She couldn't be sure who she would face if she went back there, and she might even die for her efforts.

But the alternative was that she would have to find supplies and water elsewhere, and so far, she hadn't had any luck. After the gunshot had gone off, she spent a while walking around, praying for a source of fresh water, but she was unsuccessful. She was on the opposite end of the island to the group, trying to stay out of their way, so she couldn't hope to use any of the supplies she'd gotten for them. After everything that had gone down, how was it that she was the one on the outside looking in again? How had David managed to push her out after everything he'd done?

Paranoia was quickly settling into her bones. What if they believed what David was telling them? What if they all turned on her and wanted to see her dead? If they believed she was the assassin, then she knew they wouldn't want to show her any mercy…

No, she couldn't risk that being the case. That was why she needed to keep her distance and hope that she made it through the day. Soon, there would be another task announced, and they would all have to figure out how to survive it, not just her. They'd be too preoccupied with their own survival to worry about her. She shuffled into the shade of the trees and tried not to think about how dry her mouth felt and how fast her heartbeat was.

It was about an hour later when the familiar crackle warbled over a nearby speaker. Olivia sat up attentively to listen, wondering when this had begun to feel like her norm.

"Good morning, contestants. Last night's events were certainly exciting, weren't they?" The Gamemaster let out their signature bone-chilling laugh. No matter how many times Olivia heard it, it never failed to sicken her. "Having said that, we were all very sorry to lose young Harry. Don't worry. The assassin gave him a quick death."

Olivia's heart squeezed. The poor kid. He had so much left to live for. Now, he'd never get the chance.

"Poor kid. Should have stuck to tennis, I guess! But there are still plenty of contestants out there, and there's something very exciting to play for today. We're going to have a little game of capture the flag. Somewhere on the island, we have planted a red flag that's available for anyone to take. The first person to reach it will win a very *special* prize. Do I have your attention?"

Olivia knew that whatever the Gamemaster was about to offer them would shake things up somehow. It might even turn some of the contestants against one another if the offer was particularly tempting. Still, whatever it was was less important to her now that the whole island was against her. She only hoped it would take the attention away from her.

"This task won't be a team effort. Because the person to reach the flag first and touch it will be granted the ability to leave the island for good. Sounds too good to be true, doesn't it? But this is one promise I swear I'll keep. The first person to touch the flag will be airlifted out of here by the end of the day and taken home, safe and sound. But let's be honest… an offer this tempting is definitely going to bring out some selfish intentions, right? Are you prepared to watch the others around you stab you in the back? Maybe you should be. I bet certain contestants out there are getting ready for another dose of betrayal…"

Olivia clenched her fists at her side. She knew the Gamemaster was adding fuel to the fire of the accusations against her, hoping to cause chaos. She wondered if it would work.

The flag didn't interest her, but she was interested in who might try to snatch it up. She wouldn't be surprised if David was willing to cut them all down to get to the flag first, even as a saboteur. She didn't think any of the others would do the same, but she still couldn't be sure which of them were trustworthy. They were all scared; they all wanted to go home. Any of them might be capable of trying for it.

The Gamemaster had weaved such a tangled web for them to escape, and now all she could think of was the manila folder that had information on all of the contestants. If only she'd had the chance to read about them all—then she would know who she could trust and who she couldn't. But since that was off the table, she would have to hope that David was the only backstabber in the crew.

The Gamemaster signed off, and Olivia stood shakily. She knew now that she had to try to meet the others at the flag. She would prove that she wasn't working against them. She had no interest in capturing the flag for herself, and she would be happy to allow any of the others to take it. She wanted to see someone get off the island safely, and she wanted to stay to make sure the rest of them survived. As soon as she crossed paths with them, she would make her intentions known. If David tried to throw her under the bus, then she would just have to take them to the bunker and prove to them that he was working against them. That would only strengthen her case.

But Olivia was beginning to worry that she wouldn't get that far. She was already feeling weak and dehydrated. She could survive without food for as long as she was still left on the island if she had to, but the lack of water was already sending shooting pains through her head. The wound she'd sustained on her swim to rescue Yara was throbbing, and she was worried about the fact that she hadn't changed the dressing. She could only hope that water and bandages were close by when she found the flag.

She began her trek through the woods slowly and carefully. She knew she had to preserve her energy and keep to the shade. She was already sunburned as it was. Her cheeks were beginning to blister, and the pain was hot and agonizing. Her head was throbbing, and her limbs were sore. Every step she took only made her want to sink to her knees and wait out the pain.

She shook her head. She'd already put herself through so much on the island. She couldn't give in now. She hoped that the others would see what she'd sacrificed too. She'd been the one who got them through their first challenge, who brought them together at the beach, who saved Yara during the swim. She had advised the other contestants on what to do the day before for the third challenge. Was it possible that after all that, they would still think she was untrustworthy? Would they trust David's word over hers after he ran off with their supplies? After he had effectively killed Tess?

She didn't want to believe it. Surely some of them would have her back? Maybe they had already turned David away and dismissed his words. Maybe they were hoping they'd find her as much as she hoped to find them.

But she reminded herself as well that David was armed. He had a gun, and she knew if he saw her again, he wouldn't be afraid to use it in order to silence her. He might not have spilled blood personally yet, but he seemed determined to do anything necessary to keep in the Gamemaster's good graces. If she wasn't careful, she would end up getting shot down before she had a chance to defend herself. That was something she couldn't risk. She'd have to tread carefully from now on.

She kept on stumbling through the woods, wishing desperately for a source of water. She hadn't seen many sources of fresh water on the island, and she had no doubt that was deliberate on the Gamemaster's part. They wanted the contestants to fight over the precious resources they'd been given on the first day, and they didn't care if people died in the process. Olivia cursed David for sending her away without any supplies. In that moment, it was possible that he had signed her death certificate. Would he actually care? She saw the way he had dismissed Tess's death with such ease. Maybe he really was as cruel and cold as he seemed.

The hottest part of the day was approaching, and Olivia felt no closer to finding the flag. She stopped to rest against a tree, sweat pouring from her forehead. She'd never been so desperate in her life for something as she was for water in that moment. She couldn't stop thinking about an ice-cold glass filled with water that would save her. She curled her hands into fists, telling herself to stay strong. She'd heard people talk about starvation and dehydration before, but she never imagined the pain would be so bad. It felt like her body was actively working against her, making her sweat, making her joints ache, and making her feel dizzy.

She knew she was slowly dying.

She sank to her knees for a moment, and then she worried that she might not be able to get back up. Terror squeezed at her stomach. She spent her life running from trouble, but what could she do about it this time? The only solution was water, and that was hard to come by on a desert island.

Olivia was shaking as she stood up again. She thought about her parents at home. Were they watching her crumble on the livestream? Thousands of others were. Would they look at her, sweat-coated and dirt-splattered, and think she was done for? Was anyone out there rooting for her to carry on fighting? Were they laughing at her, hoping that the strongest contestant on the island would die next? She swallowed, and her throat was scratchy and dry. Giving up wasn't an option. She wouldn't give anyone that satisfaction.

She kept on going. She felt like she was moving at a snail's pace, but she was making progress, and that was all that mattered. She kept her ears pricked for sounds of the other contestants, and her eyes blurred as she searched for signs of the red flag. At this rate, she was beginning to think about snatching the flag for herself, just so she could find water. But she pushed the selfish thoughts aside. That wasn't what she was there for. Just one bottle of water would revive her. A bottle of water and a night of rest and her friends back at her side. Was that too much to ask for? She just had to convince someone to give it to her.

That might be easier said than done.

As Olivia carried on trudging through the woods, she finally looked up and saw something fluttering a short distance away. She swallowed, wondering if she was imagining it. She was so dehydrated now that she wouldn't be shocked if she were delusional, seeing what she wanted to see. But there it was, the red flag blowing in the slight breeze. Olivia laughed desperately, almost tripping over her own feet as she began to run toward it, desperate to make it before she collapsed. Her legs were about to give out on her, but she didn't have far to go. Then she would wait at the flag for the others to find it. That was the only plan that made sense to her—

"Stop where you are, Olivia."

Olivia's heart froze. She was mere meters away from the flag. She looked up and saw the others coming from the east, all of them with their gazes fixed on her. She saw Brock, and her heart melted a little. But his face was worried, and Olivia understood what that meant.

David had brainwashed them all.

"Don't move, or I'll shoot you," David said, waving the gun at her. "What did I tell you, everyone? She was going to take the flag for herself. She knew where to find it because she's the traitor. She was going to screw you all over again. She killed Harry and—"

"I don't want the stupid flag," Olivia said, her voice raspy from the lack of water. "I don't want anything but my life. Please. I'm dehydrated. I just want some water. Then one of you can take the flag, and I can tell you what really happened."

"How do we know we can trust you?" Elodie asked, chewing her nails. "David said you cornered him. That he only got away because he managed to knock you over… he said you're working for the Gamemaster. That you were the assassin."

"It's not me. It's him," Olivia wheezed, falling to the ground. "I was with him when Harry was shot. But he's the traitor, not me. I don't know who the assassin is. Please, don't do this. How can you believe I'd turn on you all? I've helped with every single challenge. David is the one who stole from us all and turned his back on us."

"I told you all, it's a load of rubbish," Henry snapped, glaring around at the other contestants. "Olivia is the only reason we've made it this far in the first place. You only believed David because you were scared he'd turn on you all… why do you think he's the only one here with a weapon?"

"You can't be serious, now," David scoffed. He was putting on a skeptical face, but there was a hint—no, more than a hint— of fear in his eyes. "You know she's just been manipulating you, right? Gaining your trust so she can betray you."

"That's… that's not…" Olivia fell to her knees. "Please, I just need some water."

"She's lying," David pressed. "Look at the way she's faking—"

"Lower the gun, David, or I'll kill you myself," Brock said in a quiet, cold voice. But before anyone else could respond, Olivia watched Melody slam her fist into David's jaw. He recoiled and dropped the gun as he fell to the ground. Olivia's mouth fell open in shock. She hadn't been expecting that, to say the least.

Melody picked up the gun and stepped away from the group. Olivia's heart skipped a beat. Was Melody about to shoot her instead? Had her most faithful ally outside of her friends turned on her? But she soon realized it was her delusion talking when Melody put the gun on her belt and swung the backpack off her shoulder.

"You're all crazy. The woman looks like she's on death's door," Melody exclaimed. She rolled a bottle of water to Olivia who scrabbled toward it. She desperately unscrewed the bottle and drank heartily until the bottle was empty. Relief washed over her immediately, and it soothed her dry throat. She took a few deep breaths, as if somehow the lack of water had affected her lungs as well; and even though she would still need more, she would at least survive. She wouldn't die for now. Then she looked at the stunned group again. David was still on the ground, clutching his jaw, while the others stood perfectly still, as though waiting to see what might happen next. Melody turned to her once more.

"We're going to talk this out like adults," she said firmly. "Everyone gets to say their piece. And then when we're done, we'll decide who the liar is."

CHAPTER TWENTY-THREE

OLIVIA STAYED SITTING A FEW YARDS FROM THE FLAG. She had no intention of taking it for herself, but she also had no intention of allowing David to make a run for it either—not after what he'd done to them all. If anyone was going to make it off the island, it certainly wasn't going to be him. She wouldn't allow him to get away without repercussions.

But he wasn't the only one on trial. Olivia barely had the strength to stand up, but she knew she had to fight for her case, even if she could hardly speak. Melody handed her another bottle of water with an uneasy look on her face, like she wasn't quite sure how to handle the whole situation. Olivia simply sipped her water quietly and waited for someone to start the conversation.

Everyone was glancing at one another suspiciously. How had it all fallen apart so quickly?

"You stupid cow," David muttered at Melody as he nursed his bruised jaw. "You can't just go around hitting people like that."

"And you can't just go around accusing people of being traitors and pointing guns at them. Especially since we have much less reason to trust you than the person you're pointing fingers at," Melody said. "And if you try anything else, I've got another fist right here. This time, I'll break your nose."

Olivia almost smiled. It seemed that Melody had found her reason to fight after all, and now she was blossoming into a true force to be reckoned with. It was one of the reasons Olivia had warmed to her in the first place. But she knew that further violence would get them nowhere. They were only halfway through their trials, and they needed to survive together for another few days. That meant learning to get along, even with their rivals.

Melody turned to Olivia once again, her face softening. "David has told his side of the story. It's only fair that you get to speak yours."

Olivia stared at David, wondering how much detail she could go into before he would launch himself at her. She swallowed, her throat still sore from dehydration. But she would tell her version before David had the chance to muddy the waters further, and she'd tell it in full.

"I ran off alone to find a place to hide, just like everyone else did," Olivia began. "I was running out of time… and I tripped on a handle to a trapdoor. It was hidden beneath the dirt. I didn't have time to look for anywhere better, and I figured I'd be safer underground. But I found a bunker beneath the earth. Inside… well, I'm still not fully sure what was inside. I was investigating while I was on my own. I found information belonging to the Gamemaster… there were files with profiles of us all. I figured I'd be able to find out who the spies were, but I never got a chance to finish looking. David came down into the bunker. I had a gun that I found in the bunker, but he was also armed with a gun. He told me that he was a saboteur, but not the assassin. I can confirm that, considering we were together when Harry was shot. He can't have been far away… but I knew someone was dead when only one shot sounded out."

The group began to mutter among themselves. Elodie and Clementine shuffled away from David, who was now glaring at the entire group. Olivia swallowed, continuing her story.

"He allowed me to leave, but he told me that he was going to return to the group and accuse me of the things he's been doing since he arrived here. He agreed to work for the Gamemaster because he was promised money and an experimental treatment for an incurable cancer. He had nothing to lose if he died here and everything to gain. So, he went to extreme lengths to make sure he'd be on the Gamemaster's good side—including sending me away with no food or water, despite there being plenty in the bunker."

"And so, he was willing to let any of us die for his glory?" Brock asked, shaking with anger. David took one look around him at the sea of angry contestants and scrambled to his feet. He tried to make a run for the flag, but before he made it more than a few steps, Henry grabbed the back of his shirt and yanked him back, toppling the pair of them over. They wrestled on the ground for a moment, and Melody aimed the gun right at David's forehead.

Olivia's heart jolted in her chest. "No!" she shouted. She stumbled to her feet and moved toward Melody unsteadily, trying to hold her back. It was taking all the energy she had left, but she was determined that no one else would get hurt.

"Don't do it. Please. We don't need to kill anyone. Look at what we've been put through already. The Gamemaster wants us to turn on each other. Don't let them win. Remember that we're being watched."

Melody was shaking a little, but she lowered the gun slowly. She shook her head. She handed the gun to Olivia. "Take… take it away from me. I don't want to be responsible for what I'm tempted to do. And I'm going to take your actions as further proof that the only liar we have here is David," she said, glaring down at him. "You almost had us fooled. I should never have trusted you. I'm so sorry, Olivia."

"It's okay. Things are more than a little tense around here," Olivia said, trying to keep her voice level. "But we don't need to hurt one another any longer. David… you don't need to do this. If you're willing to give up the fight, we can take you back again. You can come back to the group and ride this out with us until it's all over."

"Are you insane?" Henry barked. "He would happily have killed you five minutes ago. He's already responsible for Tess's death. We can't trust this man while he's still alive."

"I'm not letting any harm come to him. It's not how this is going to go," Olivia said as calmly as she could muster. "We've been thrown into one of the most messed-up situations I could possibly imagine. He did what he thought he needed to in order to survive. And yes, greed blinded him. Yes, he did bad things for what he wanted. But none of us are perfect. He was a desperate man. He wanted another chance at life. And the Gamemaster promised it to him. But David… don't you want to prove yourself as an honest man? Show your children that you're not a cruel person? Show them that you can change?"

David was trembling as he stared up at Olivia. She didn't want to get too close in case he did something rash, but she stepped closer to him and bent down to his level. He eyed her up suspiciously.

"Why?" he asked her. She frowned at him.

"Why what?"

"Why would you show me mercy? After everything I've done? You don't even know the half of the things I've done, the people I've hurt… and you're willing to put it behind you. Why?"

Olivia swallowed. That wasn't an easy question to answer, but she was willing to give it a try. She didn't care if the world was watching. If she had a chance to talk David down, to balance things out again, then she would do it. Maybe the people back home would see that there was more than one way to deal with hate and evil.

"I see a lot of death in my line of work. I see a lot of deceit and treachery and cruelty. It can be tempting to feel like it's personal when you get too involved in a case," Olivia said. "But when you've seen enough lives collapse, you start to realize that life is precious. *All* life. I've lost a lot in my life. My sister was murdered a few years ago. My mom went missing, and I went through all the stages of grief, believing I'd lost her forever. I look into the eyes of killers and know that they feel no mercy when they end a life. They don't care that the person they're hurting has a family back home, or that someone who cares about them is waiting to hear from them. They're just happy to end someone's life and be done with it. It's cold and unfeeling. And I don't see that in you. I mean, I don't see goodness, but I don't see evil either."

David stared at her, his expression hard. Olivia continued, her throat raw from talking.

"I've come face to face with death a hundred times. Plenty of people have wished me dead. I'm still standing, and I intend to stay that way. A few times I've gotten myself out. Other times I've gotten lucky. But I've never been in a position where someone has been pointing a gun at me and happily let me go. I know why you didn't kill me back in the bunker, David. You never wanted to in the first place. You would've won more points if you'd ended my life, but it was never something you considered, was it? You were happy to do a lot of things to please the Gamemaster, but killing me, or anyone else, wasn't one of them. Because even though you've done bad things, you're redeemable. You'd never kill an innocent. You'd never be able to pull the trigger on any one of us."

"You don't know that," David said, but his voice trembled as he spoke, and there were tears stinging his eyes. Olivia's eyes softened.

"I do. You had the upper hand here just before. You were the only one armed. You could've shot us all. You could've gone back to the camp and killed every last person before they had a chance to react. One sign of them not agreeing with you, and you could've killed them. But you didn't. Because you don't want to. So, you won't."

A tear slid down David's papery cheek, his eyes trained on the ground. Somehow, he looked like a child. An innocent child who didn't understand how he'd gotten himself in so much trouble. Olivia was tempted to feel sorry for him, even after everything he'd done. He was a small, lonely man with not much to live for. She could see how he'd clutched at one last way to feel good about himself before he left the world. He wanted to feel like he mattered. And that was a feeling Olivia knew all too well.

"Olivia, this is all very well and good," Henry said softly. "But if he can stab us in the back once, he can do it again. We can't just let him wander around the island because he's showing the slightest bit of remorse."

"I agree," Olivia said, straightening up. "We can find a way to keep him from harming anyone. And then when we make it home, the police will deal with him however is necessary. That will be their problem."

David's head snapped up to look at Olivia. "What?"

Olivia frowned. "You conspired with the Gamemaster to harm the other contestants. You did it before even coming here without any coercion. That's breaking the law, and you know it. You'll face charges when we're back on American soil."

David's face sunk in horror. Olivia knew she shouldn't have said anything in that moment. She had just let David know that a change of heart wasn't going to do him any good now. He would be just as well siding with the Gamemaster still. He'd live out the rest of his days in a cell. She could see the cogs turning inside his mind.

"David… don't do anything rash," Olivia warned him. She was scared that he might try and hurt someone again.

But she never expected what he did next.

In a flash, he shoved something deep into his own chest. Olivia cried out as she saw that it was a knife he'd produced from his pocket. He gasped, blood coating his lips as he fell onto the ground, grunting in pain. Olivia kneeled beside him, trying to staunch the flow of the blood, but she already knew it was too late to save David. He groaned in pain, but he twisted the knife deeper, making Olivia recoil a little. There was nothing left for her to do but watch the life leave him.

"Why did you do that?" Olivia whispered, several involuntary tears escaping her eyes. David looked her directly in the eyes as the color drained from his face.

"Because… because if I didn't do it to myself, I would've done it to you," he croaked. And then he closed his eyes for the final time.

Olivia was hit by a wave of exhaustion that made her press her face to the ground. After everything they'd endured, this was her final straw. She felt gentle hands on her back. Brock's hands. But even he couldn't reach inside her at that moment and soothe the pain. She had tried so hard to make things right.

But some people just couldn't be fixed.

CHAPTER TWENTY-FOUR

It took Olivia some time to be able to move away from David's still body. She wasn't processing what had happened very well, and she knew that she was nearing her limit of what she could cope with. The island was designed to push them, but she had been pushed farther than any of them combined. She had thrown herself at every challenge, and it had still backfired on her so many times. It was almost as if the Gamemaster's sole intention was to make her entire life a misery.

And now another man was dead. He might have been the bad apple of the bunch, but Olivia didn't want to see him die. She had hoped he might redeem himself and prove he wasn't bad at his core. But those words he'd told her as he died would never leave her.

If I didn't do it to myself, I would've done it to you.

Melody put an arm around Olivia's shoulders and guided her away from David's body. Olivia tried to remember how to breathe, how to push the awfulness of it all to the back of her head. But David's dead eyes kept staring back at her in her mind.

If I didn't do it to myself, I would've done it to you.

"We still have to decide who takes the flag," she said gently to Olivia. "We decided this morning that it might be best to put it to a vote. Is that all right with you?"

Olivia swallowed back her tears and nodded. It seemed like a fair way to do it. She could see that Elodie and Clementine were eyeing up the flag, but she was convinced that neither of them would make a run for it. They wouldn't be willing to leave the other behind. And that meant that Olivia was pretty sure that none of them would take the flag now without permission. The remaining members of the group weren't that selfish.

They all gathered close to it, staring at the flag that could save one of their lives. Olivia sniffed and turned to the group.

"Does anyone want to say anything to make their case?" Olivia asked the group. "I'll be staying regardless. I don't want to take away someone's opportunity to get out of here."

"Me too," Brock said firmly.

"And me," Henry agreed. The others were silent, looking shiftily at one another. Olivia understood that it was hard to commit to not leaving the island at that very moment. After the horrors they'd been put through, it was easy to see an easy way out and want to take it. Elodie, Clementine, Yara, Melody and Rose could walk away without any more fear if they were chosen.

But Melody folded her arms around herself, turning her back on the flag. Olivia knew then that her new friend would be staying.

"I'll stay too," Melody said. "And I think that it's clear who should get to leave. Rose is carrying a child. We'll be saving two lives instead of just one."

"Melody…" Rose began softly, but Melody held her hand up to stop her.

BEHIND CLOSED DOORS

"It has to be you, Rose. You're not fit to continue in any of the tasks. You've been pushing your body too much as it is."

Elodie nodded. "She should be on bed rest, not trying to survive on a desert island. Why are we even debating this at this point? She should be the one who leaves the island."

"Or Yara," Brock chimed in. "She's sick. I agree with you, I really do… but I'm worried for Yara too. She's been battling hard with her withdrawals, but she should really be getting professional help…"

"I'm okay," Yara said, though she hadn't stopped shivering the entire time they'd been gathered at the flag. "Melody is right. Rose should be the one to go. She should never have been here in the first place. And we all want her baby to have a chance at life, right? That's not something we can talk about any longer. I vote for Rose to go too."

Rose's eyes were filled with tears, her hands protectively placed on her belly.

"I can't… I can't just leave…"

"Yes, you can," Olivia insisted. "Think of your future, Rose. Think of your child's future. We'll be saving two lives, not just one. And no one is more deserving of another chance at life than you. It makes sense."

"And truly, no offense to you, Rose, but you're not exactly helpful to these tasks," Henry said. "You can barely walk at the moment. The team will function best if we're all at our strongest. If you go, you'll give us all a better chance at living."

"Not very tactfully put, but I agree," Brock said. "And if Yara thinks she is well enough to stay… I think she's a safer bet. You don't need to feel guilty, Rose. This is what we're all choosing. Right?"

"Yes," Clementine said with a nod.

"I think so," Elodie agreed, though her eyes still rested on the flag. Still, she made no move to take it. The rest of the group murmured their assent. Rose sniffed, holding her arms around herself.

"I… I can't thank you all enough. I thought… I thought I'd never make it off this island alive."

"You deserve to have a chance at life," Olivia told her gently. "I'll feel better knowing you are safe. I think we all will. And maybe when we get out of this place… you can let us meet your baby."

"I'd like that," Rose said, tears now flowing freely down her face. "And I'll never forget what you all did for me. You kept me alive when I had nothing to offer you in return. Especially you, Olivia. I'll always be so grateful to you. I'm so sorry you've had to suffer so much… I wish we had all known better. You saved us all so many times."

"That's what I'm here for," Olivia said, her heart squeezing in her chest. As much as the pain of what had just happened to David still rested inside her, she was glad to be able to save someone for once. This was possibly the only moment they'd spent on the island where something good was happening.

"How precious," the Gamemaster's voice droned from a speaker. "But hurry it up. We're all dying of boredom over here."

Rose sniffed and turned to the flag. She looked like she was about to step up to it, but then she threw her arms around Olivia in a hug. One by one, the other contestants moved to embrace her, too, all of them wrapped up in one big hug. Olivia closed her eyes for a moment. She hoped their show of love would anger the Gamemaster. She hoped that their show of humanity would remind the people watching that they were people too. They'd been put through hell, but they wouldn't let it break them down. Not the way it broke David. Not the way the Gamemaster hoped it would break them.

They were only growing stronger.

When they finally let Rose go, she took a deep breath and walked up to the flag. When she wrapped her hand around the pole, there was a look of triumph in her eyes. Olivia couldn't help but smile. Finally, they had a win. Finally, something good had come of everything on the island.

Soon after, armed guards came to collect David and Rose. Rose waved goodbye to them all anxiously as she was taken away. Olivia could only pray that the Gamemaster was true to their word, that they'd look after Rose now. Soon enough, Rose should be on her way back home to safety. She hoped that no matter how

FATAL GAMES

cruel the Gamemaster was, they'd have mercy on a sweet, young woman like Rose.

The remainder of the group silently began to trudge back to their camp, exhaustion and sadness settling into their hearts. They were close to the end now, but not close enough for Olivia's liking. She just wanted them all to make it. Their group was so small now compared to at the beginning. They'd lost so many; Clive, Tess, Harry, David, and now Rose. It was enough to make Olivia's stomach twist. She couldn't face another loss, and she didn't think the others could either.

They would just have to try even harder to survive, no matter what.

CHAPTER TWENTY-FIVE

OLIVIA WAS RELIEVED WHEN THEY ALL MADE IT BACK TO camp. The sight of the supply boxes and the pitched tents almost made her cry with joy. She'd only been away for a day and a half, and yet she had thought she might never return.

She immediately sat down by the fire and helped herself to some of the rations. They had a rationing system in place, but she didn't see any reason to regard it considering she hadn't eaten in a day and a half. If anyone had anything to say to her about it, they'd have to face her first. Considering they'd been willing to turn on her, she didn't care much what they thought in that moment.

She hadn't realized how hungry she was until she started to eat. She had been so focused on how thirsty she'd been that her hunger had come second. Now, she had to stop herself from eating everything left in their supply box. She caught Elodie watching her in slight disgust, and she felt hot anger slice through her like a knife. How dare Elodie judge her? She'd been through a lot that day. She could've died. Elodie had been happy to allow Olivia to take risks on her behalf for days. She could at least show some respect for her now that she'd returned.

Olivia took a breath and calmed herself. No, this wasn't right. She didn't know what the others had been through either. She couldn't fall into the same selfish trap David had.

She didn't feel much like talking to anyone, so she walked down to the beach alone. She had been through enough emotions for one day. The stress of it all was weighing heavy on her, and she needed some time to just process everything that had happened. Being around the people who had almost betrayed her wasn't going to make her feel any better.

She stared out at the open water, dreaming of quiet, quaint Belle Grove. It felt so out of reach, so far in her past that she could barely picture what it was like there. Time on the island was having a funny effect on her. She hugged her knees to her chest as she sat on the sand. She could finally admit to herself that she was terrified. Every single day felt like it might be her last. She felt paranoid, like anyone could turn on her at any moment. She felt let down by the others who were so willing to take David's side even after everything he'd done. She understood that allegiances here were fluid—that they changed all the time like the ocean tides—but she'd done nothing but protect these people. The fact that they were so untrusting of her made her wonder how much of the suffering she'd been through was really worth it.

Olivia heard footsteps coming through the trees and turned to see who it was. She was expecting Brock or Melody, but she was surprised to see that it was Yara. She was carrying the first aid kit from the supply crates, and she sat down beside Olivia on the sand, unpacking several supplies.

"You need to change your dressing. And that sunburn on your face is pretty nasty," she said. "I think there's some aloe vera in here."

"Does it look bad?"

Yara laughed. "Well, it doesn't look good, I'll be honest with you. Not exactly Hollywood-level skincare here."

Olivia tried for a smile, but the effort of it felt too much, and it hurt when she stretched the tender skin on her cheek. Yara carefully dabbed some lotion on the peeling skin.

"I never really thanked you… for what you did for me," she said gently. "I don't know many people who would risk their life like that to help me."

Olivia sighed. "I wasn't just going to leave you out there, Yara. What kind of person would I be if I did?"

"That's the thing about you, Olivia. You assume everyone thinks the same way you do. When in reality, most people would just accept that I was a goner. But you always put everyone else before you, don't you?"

Olivia sighed again. She couldn't explain where all of her frustrations had sprung up from, but now they refused to leave her alone. They were cutting her deep, and it was making it impossible to feel comfortable with any of her teammates. "I try to look out for people. But sometimes I wonder why I do it. The world still keeps fighting against me, and I always end up on my back foot."

"Girl, the world picks battles with us all. Maybe not the same ones, but we're all fighting demons somewhere along the way. It builds character. And, well, yeah, you do have a lot of trouble in your life. But that's because of who you are. Because you dedicate your job and your life to helping others. Not because you're not trying hard enough. I admire you, Olivia. You never stop fighting. I could never live your life. Absolutely could not be me. I'm much more suited to the silver screen."

Olivia closed her eyes. She appreciated that Yara was apparently in good enough spirits to try to cheer her up, but she couldn't laugh. "It's getting more and more tempting to stop. To just let it overwhelm me for good."

"Don't give up," Yara said, lowering her voice. "It's what the Gamemaster wants. You can't let that happen."

Olivia nodded slightly. She knew she couldn't afford to truly fall apart when cameras were watching her every move. In the heat of certain moments, she could almost forget they were there. But Yara was right. If the Gamemaster had eyes on them, she had to appear like she wasn't falling apart, even if she was.

"Brock was so worried about you when you didn't come back to camp," Yara continued, finishing up with the aloe cream. "He kept going off in search of you in the woods. Henry too. It was driving David crazy."

Olivia smiled slightly. "Brock will always come for me. It's in his nature."

"You're so lucky. I guess back when we dated, I never really saw him the way he is now. But I wonder if that's because he changed for you. Maybe if we were still together now, he would be a different man. I don't think he would've gone to the ends of the earth for me the way he would for you."

"I wouldn't be so sure, Yara. We're here, aren't we? We came to make sure you were okay. That was his idea."

Yara smiled. "I guess you're right. But you bring out something special in him, Olivia. Something I never could. You're a good match. I like seeing you together. It gives me hope that someday, I might find someone too. Although it feels less likely these days."

"Don't say that, Yara."

"It's true. Here I am, being live streamed all over the world… and all my flaws are right there for everyone to see. So much for my carefully curated public image," she whispered. Olivia's expression softened. She had to be talking about her alcohol problem. Even now, days into her withdrawals, Yara was shaking hard, and her skin was as pale as the moon in the sky. She was a mess, but Olivia still saw beyond that. She was a good person. She didn't deserve to put herself down like that.

"You're doing great, Yara," Olivia told her quietly. "It's like you said… we all have our battles to fight, right? And you're not giving up. And in my book, that's admirable."

Olivia swore she could see Yara's lip quivering, but she kept her head dipped, her hair falling in front of her face. "Thanks, Olivia. At least I know someone sees me that way." She swallowed and forced a smile. Even despite the dirt smeared on her face and her heavily lidded eyes, somehow that Hollywood magic kicked in. For a moment, she was the old Yara. Glitz and glam and all. "Well. Shall we head back to camp? I think Brock will be missing us."

Olivia chuckled and stood up, then helped Yara to her feet. She didn't say anything else, but she silently thanked Yara for bringing her out of her funk a little. It seemed like she knew exactly what to say to make things better.

And at least she had one true friend to rely on.

CHAPTER TWENTY-SIX

Day five was upon them, and it came with a dose of anxiety that had the islanders on edge. The group was quiet and solemn, nibbling on some of the meager supplies they had left to give them strength for the day. It was becoming clearer that their survival was getting harder—their group was shrinking, and so were their supplies. They didn't have to fight for much longer, and yet the island was dragging them all down.

The only person in the group who appeared a little brighter was Yara. She didn't look quite so pale anymore, and she was eating properly for the first time since they'd found her. She finished up a protein bar and even licked the wrapper, tossing it back into the too-rapidly emptying supply box.

"I think I'm ready for whatever they throw at us today," she told the group as she unwrapped and munched on a granola bar. Rationing seemed to have gone completely out the window since Olivia's return, but she didn't have the energy to enforce it again. "I'm definitely feeling better than I was."

"You look better too. No offense… you looked kind of zombielike before," Henry said. Yara sniffed and twirled her hair around her finger.

"Well, I appreciate it. Desert island chic must suit me. It's bringing back the color in my cheeks, huh?"

No one was in the mood for jokes, least of all Olivia. Even after Yara's brief pep talk on the beach, she couldn't help feeling the doom and gloom. She closed her eyes for a moment to block the world out. Just three more days and they'd all get to go home. That was if they didn't die before then, and if the Gamemaster was true to their word of letting them all go at the end. For all she knew, they'd be stuck there forever, completing tasks until they dropped dead for the Gamemaster's entertainment.

"Don't we usually have some instructions by now?" Melody asked. Olivia looked up at the sky and saw that the sun was almost at its highest. She was right. Normally by now, they were well on their way with a new challenge. It made her feel uneasy. How hadn't she noticed that? She clearly wasn't at the top of her game.

"Perhaps this task will take place at nighttime," Clementine suggested.

"Or perhaps we are meant to go and look for clues to the task ourselves. Like a treasure hunt," Elodie mused.

The comment seemed to set everyone around the campfire on edge, and Olivia understood why. If they were meant to look for the task somewhere on the island, then they needed to get moving. It was nearing midday, which was eating into task time. Olivia didn't know what would happen if they somehow missed out on the task, but she was sure it couldn't be a good thing. She chewed her thumb. She knew the others would be looking to her to lead the way once again. She should say something. Even in her low mood, she was willing to be a leader if she had to be.

"Maybe a few of us could go and hunt around the island for some ideas," Olivia suggested. Then she paused, thinking about the bunker. Now that David was gone, perhaps she could return there and get some answers. Maybe they wouldn't need to complete the task at all. Maybe they could find an alternative way off the island. If there were answers, they were in that bunker. A plan began to form in her mind. She realized just how much she wanted to go back there.

"I also think that I'd like to return to the bunker where David found me," Olivia told the group. She was past the point of deliberating if she could trust them all. Half of them were her friends, and the other half were becoming fast allies. She might not trust the twins so much, but the rest of them she knew she could rely on.

"Why would you want to go back there? After what happened there?" Yara asked, frowning. "Isn't it dangerous?"

"Because there was information down there. And food and water," Olivia said in a low voice. She didn't want the cameras to pick up what she was saying if she could help it. "I think there might be things down there that might help us get off the island. And what else do we have to do, really? There's no challenge so far. We can sit here twiddling our thumbs, or we can do something to try to save ourselves. I know which I'd rather do."

The twins began to murmur to one another, sounding intrigued by the idea. Melody nodded firmly.

"All right. I'm in, definitely. I'll come with you."

"Great. Maybe one more person?" Olivia asked, looking around the group. Both Henry and Brock looked like they were about to speak, but Yara got there first.

"I'll come. Anything to get back at the Gamemaster for what they did to me," she said, her expression hardening. Olivia nodded decisively.

"All right then, looks like we've got a squad. The rest of you, are you willing to take a look around the island and see if there's anything going on?"

"Sure," Brock said. "But don't be gone for too long in case we need to do something for the task. Let's meet back here in an hour or two? Is that enough time for you to get to the bunker and take a look around? Or do you need longer?"

"I think it should be enough time," Olivia said. She guessed she could always return when she needed to. She thought about the hidden weapons in the basement, and her stomach twisted. If she could find a gun again, then it would change the game for them. They would be able to defend themselves, maybe even take matters into their own hands. It was worth a shot.

"Let's get moving," Melody said, standing up and brushing herself off. "I'll grab us a few supplies just in case we're out there longer than expected. Then we can go."

As Melody began to pack up a bag, Olivia headed over to check in on Brock. Every time she left him, it felt like a gut punch. She had a not-so-irrational fear that she wouldn't make it back to him every time. After the last few days, nothing was out of the realm of possibility. She cupped his cheek.

"Be safe," she told him. He smiled at her.

"Don't worry about me. Worry about yourself, my troublemaker," he murmured. Olivia gave him a quick peck on the lips, not wanting to linger too long. She didn't want it to feel like she was saying goodbye. She would make her way back to him soon enough.

"Where's mine, American?" Henry teased, puckering his lips. Olivia swatted his arm playfully.

"You'll get a kiss from my knuckles if you're not careful," she said with a grin. He laughed, but then Henry's smile quickly turned to concern, and he reached out to her for a hug, which she accepted quickly. She understood his fears—he was having the same thoughts that she was. The farther into the games they got, the more uncertain each day felt. If they were going their separate ways, they had to hope it wasn't for the last time.

"Take care of the others, and yourself," Henry told her. Olivia nodded against his shoulder.

"Same to you," she said. She was glad Henry was there to watch Brock's back. In fact, she was less worried about their group than she was about her own. Not only was her group smaller, but Yara was very much the liability of their leftover squad. Melody could handle herself, at least, but it still didn't feel great going off without Brock or Henry at her side.

Still, she trusted herself. Where they were going might be dangerous, she knew. If the Gamemaster saw her going back there, they might have obstacles in mind for her. But that was a bridge she'd cross when she reached it. She just had to take action and hope it paid off.

Without too much more fuss, the two groups separated to begin their treks. Olivia led the way back to the bunker, trying to remember the route she had taken in her panic to hide from the assassin. She glanced at Melody as she thought about Harry's death that day. They hadn't had much of a chance to catch up since the two groups had been reunited, and Melody had seemed close with Harry from the beginning. She thought it was about time she checked in on her.

"You holding up okay?" Olivia asked Melody gently. "I know you and Harry seemed to be friendly."

Melody's face darkened, and she stared straight ahead as they walked. "I'm okay, I guess," she said. "It's just… such a horrible way to go. I keep thinking about how afraid he must've been. How alone he would've felt. He spent his last hours with nobody there to talk to, to make him feel comfortable. When I was alone, hiding in the woods… I realized that would be my worst nightmare. Dying without a friend at my side. I think he would've felt that way too."

Olivia nodded in understanding. Yara was quiet, averting her gaze. Olivia guessed she didn't know Melody well enough to really get involved in the conversation. Olivia placed a hand on Melody's shoulder and guided her onward.

"There's nothing that can make any of it better," Olivia said quietly. "None of this should ever have been allowed to happen. But there's nothing any of us could've done. We were at the Gamemaster's mercy that day more than most. They left us no choice but to split off and try to save ourselves."

"I know. I don't feel guilty about what happened," Melody said. She wrapped her arms around herself. "But there's something that makes me feel ten times worse."

"What is it?"

Melody swallowed. "Well… I just keep thinking… *thank God it wasn't me.* That's terrible, isn't it? I can barely believe thoughts like that crossed my mind."

"No, it's not so terrible," Olivia said quietly. How many times had she been grateful for her own life, even if someone else's was traded out for it? Humans all had a selfish desire to cling to the life they were given. That wasn't wrong. It was just in their nature.

"It was a game of luck," Yara said quietly. "The assassin had to take out whoever they found first, no matter who it was. It just… well, it could have been any one of us."

"I would've tried to fight. I would have had to. Like you said, Olivia," Melody sniffed. "At least… I hope I would have." Her mask of bravery fell a little. She was trying hard to be strong, but everyone has their limits. In their short time on the island, Melody had really stepped up. But all it took was one stroke of bad luck before it all came tumbling down.

"And you would be right to," Olivia said with a nod. "The assassin made their choice to hurt us. We would've been within our rights to take them out first."

Silence fell upon the group, and it made the woods feel much more eerie than before. Olivia pressed onward, wishing they'd never brought up the subject in the first place. It felt too raw and real to talk about when they were still being hunted for sport by the Gamemaster. Still, there had been no announcement. Olivia had no idea why not, but it didn't make her feel any more comfortable.

They weren't far from the bunker, and Olivia was beginning to recognize her surroundings. Melody sniffed the air suspiciously, frowning.

"Does anyone else smell smoke, or is it just me?"

Olivia sniffed the air. Melody was right. It smelled like something was burning close by. Olivia looked to the sky and saw through the trees that smoke was billowing upward…

In the direction they were headed.

"No way…" Olivia murmured and set off at a run. She had to see for herself what was going on, but she already had a feeling what she'd find.

"Olivia, wait up!" Melody cried after her, but Olivia had to get to the bunker. She had to see if everything there had really gone up in smoke.

She came to a halt when she saw that she was too late. The trapdoor to the bunker was propped open, and tongues of flame flickered beneath the ground. The bunker was burning, and it was no accident. Olivia let out a sigh, shaking her head in defeat. Someone had gone there to burn the evidence left inside. She was too late to stop it.

"Olivia!"

Olivia whipped her head around at Melody's strangled cry. To her complete horror, she saw Yara holding Melody back. They were both trembling a little, but Yara's grip on Melody was like iron.

She had a knife to her throat.

"You shouldn't have come back here," Yara whispered.

CHAPTER TWENTY-SEVEN

"What the hell are you doing, Yara? Let her go," Olivia said, her voice trembling with rage. She couldn't believe that Yara would turn on any of them. What was she doing and why?

Was she one of the saboteurs?

"I... I can't tell you anything," Yara said, her voice wobbling. She didn't seem like a ruthless cutthroat traitor, and yet there she was, holding Melody hostage without any signs of letting go. Melody's face had hardened in anger, and Olivia had to hope she wouldn't try anything rash and get herself killed. One wrong move and that knife would slice through Melody's throat like butter.

FATAL GAMES

"Then where do we go from here, Yara? You're holding a knife to her throat. You do realize what you're doing, don't you? How this will change everything?"

"Everything has already changed. It's too late to go back now," Yara whispered. Olivia tried to take a step forward, but Yara yanked Melody back a few paces. Melody cried out as the knife nicked her skin ever so slightly. Olivia's heart skipped a beat or two. Yara was even more on edge than she'd imagined.

"It's never too late. It's never too late… I promise you. You haven't hurt anyone yet. You can still stop this…"

A tear trickled down Yara's cheek. "You have no idea what I have and haven't done, Olivia. I'm going to need you to follow me now. If you try anything, I'll… I'll kill her. And don't tell me I can't do it, because I can. I don't want to, but I will if you don't behave."

"All right… we'll do as you ask. There's no need for anyone to get hurt," Olivia said gently. Melody's eyes were filled with fear and anger as they met Olivia's, but she gave the young woman a warning look, telling her not to do anything too fast. Olivia still didn't understand what they were dealing with or why. Yara's motives were still completely foggy to Olivia, and she had to understand them before she could deal with the situation at hand.

"No talking from this moment forward," Yara said, swallowing down her evident nerves. "If we see the others and you try to call for help, Melody dies. If you do anything that I tell you not to…"

"I think we get the picture," Melody spat, her words like fire. "Do what you're going to do and be quick about it."

Yara nodded for Olivia to walk, and so she did. Away from the burning bunker and back toward the beaches. Her legs were wobbling as she walked, Yara occasionally barking out an instruction. How could Yara turn on them this way? The Yara she knew was a sweet woman. Sure, she had her issues, but not like this. What had happened to her to make her so cruel? There was no doubt she was a pawn for the Gamemaster, but why? What could she possibly get out of it?

She wished that Yara would speak to her, but it was becoming clearer to Olivia that it made sense not to cross her. She might not be as strong as her or Melody, but she was wilder, and that scared Olivia. She didn't want to see Melody die for her reckless actions.

It wasn't lost on her either that Yara's voice was firmer and her hands weren't shaking as bad anymore. She was still undoubtedly going through withdrawals, but the symptoms had lessened considerably.

Or had the symptoms been an act all along? Olivia couldn't be sure.

As they neared the beach, Olivia saw that there was a speedboat waiting for them on the shore. There were two armed women waiting there and a driver. Yara nodded to Olivia and then to the boat.

"Get on. If you try anything, you'll be shot."

"Doesn't it look like I'm being cooperative, Yara?" Olivia snapped at her, wading out into the water and clambering aboard the boat. At this point, she was furious. She'd faced betrayals before, but this one hurt more than most. She thought Yara was her friend. How was she ever supposed to trust anyone again when Yara was capable of turning on her? After all they'd been through. After all she'd done for her. She'd risked her life to save her more than once.

Now she was starting to wonder why she bothered at all.

Yara forced Melody onto the boat, and she took a seat next to Olivia. Their hands fumbled for one another's, and Olivia felt a little better, knowing she could at least comfort Melody now. Yara sat opposite them, her knife still in her shaking hands, but it looked like her part in it all might be over. She caught Olivia's eye briefly and then looked away, ashamed to even look at her. *Good,* Olivia thought, *I hope you never forgive yourself for this.*

Melody fumed quietly beside Olivia as the boat set off into open water. Olivia had no idea where they might be going, but watching the island disappear before her eyes was almost a relief. She had wanted to get off the island, after all. But her heart pummeled harder when she remembered that Brock and Henry and the twins were still out there. Had they been captured too? Did they even realize that Olivia and Melody were missing? Probably not.

And the worst thing was, they had no idea that they'd been betrayed. Olivia stared stonily at Yara, hoping that she would squirm underneath her gaze. Brock was going to be crushed when he realized that she wasn't who they believed her to be.

"Award-winning performance, Yara," Olivia hissed at her. Yara looked like she was going to say something, but she simply hung her head and remained quiet. Clearly, she had some remorse, but not enough. Not enough to stop her from betraying her friends.

Olivia turned to see where the speedboat was heading to. She caught a glimpse of what almost looked like a cruise ship or yacht up ahead before the guard poked her in the back with a gun, forcing her to turn back around. Salt water stung her eyes and skin as it sprayed up around them, the speedboat roaring as it bounced along the waves. She knew now where they were going.

They were going to see the Gamemaster.

Olivia was looking forward to going face to face with the person who had ruined so many lives. She would have no mercy for the Gamemaster, the way they had no mercy for her and her friends. And when she was done with the Gamemaster, she would make sure Yara paid for what she'd done too.

Anger sat low in her stomach, painful and prominent. Yara may as well have stabbed her in the gut and twisted the knife. It might've hurt less. She hoped she would at least get a chance to hear what Yara thought was worth this kind of betrayal. What was the price she had accepted to turn on the few people in her life who had her back?

But she had to concentrate on what was coming next. She didn't understand why the Games had been cut short. Were the FBI closing in on the Gamemaster? Olivia hoped that they hadn't decided to get involved—that decision might cost them their lives. The thought only fueled her frustration further. It was red hot and continuing to burn inside her. She thought they had everything handled on the island.

How wrong she'd been.

She was silent and cold as they boarded the cruise liner. Melody held on to her hand hard, and no one stopped her, which Olivia was glad for. Melody was her anchor, reminding her not to allow her anger to take over. If it did, she would lose her temper—and her focus—entirely.

The guards guided Olivia and Melody through the ship, Yara trailing at the back behind them. Olivia could hear a low murmur of chattering voices somewhere on the ship, and they seemed to be getting closer to it. It sounded like the boat was pretty packed. But for what purpose?

She would soon find out. A double set of doors opened before her, and she was pushed into a grand ballroom. The room was set up cabaret style with round tables. Crystal chandeliers hung above the heads of hundreds of guests, all of them dressed to the nines in black tie attire. Their heads turned as Olivia and Melody entered, and they began to applaud. It was a jarring experience, so much so that it felt like a dream. Olivia was forced to stand there with Melody, both of them dirty from five days in the sweltering heat on the island, while clean-cut people all around them applauded. She understood who they were right away.

They were the audience of the Games.

"Welcome, Melody and Olivia," a booming voice said. Olivia's eyes were drawn to a stage at the head of the room. There was a red curtain covering it, and the Gamemaster stood in front of it, mask still obscuring their face and identity. Yara had been right—the Gamemaster was short. But now Olivia understood that Yara was much better acquainted with the Gamemaster than she had ever let on.

"We're so glad to have you here for our special detour from the Island Games," the Gamemaster continued. "We had to adapt to certain situations outside of our control. But hey, we intend to go out with a bang! Isn't that right, everyone?"

The audience applauded once again, and Olivia stared around at the sea of faces, their eyes hollow and glinting, their smiles empty and menacing. Men and women she'd never met who had spent the best part of a week being entertained by their near-death experiences. Olivia vowed to remember as many faces as possible, in case she got out of there alive.

She would take down every single one of them.

"Wow, such a warm welcome for our contestants! You two should be proud. You're fan favorites on this boat. Everyone was rooting for the two of you."

Olivia caught sight of two large screens on either side of the stage. They seemed to be playing some kind of highlight reel of their time on the island. Olivia could barely believe she was watching herself suffering on loop. She watched the moment where she won the bounty on the first day transition into her fighting for her life underneath the waves, her head split open and Yara clinging to her like she was a life vest. Olivia turned to glare at Yara, who seemed to have shrunk off into the shadows. She would never forget how Yara had let them all down, for as long as she lived.

But she knew that might not be for much longer.

The boat was filled with people willing to see her die. Hollow, soulless people, who didn't care about anything but their own sick gratification of watching others suffer. And there were so many of them. Even if she somehow fought back, she'd never escape this room. She only had Melody to help her, and neither of them were armed.

She knew it was unlikely they'd live to see another day.

"I suppose you're wondering what we have in store for you now," the Gamemaster continued, walking across the stage. Olivia could tell that they were enjoying hosting the show. "Well, we have something very exciting for you... including a special guest! But first, we should reintroduce our other contestants. Curtains!"

Applause thundered in Olivia's ears once again as the red curtain parted to reveal four chairs on the stage. Tied to each, bound and gagged, were Olivia's other friends: Henry, Elodie, Clementine...

Brock...

She wanted to run to him. He looked like he had been beaten pretty badly. She'd seen him in much worse shape, but he also looked like he was about to pass out. His eyes met hers from across the room, and her heart sank.

Had he given up?

The others seemed like they were in a similar defeated mood. Elodie and Clementine were teary-eyed, and Henry was staring blankly into space. Olivia wondered what on earth had happened to them while they'd been separated. At least she knew that none of them were turncoats, given that they were all tied up. But after Yara's betrayal of the century, could she even be sure of that?

"Ladies and gentlemen, you've seen it all. You've watched the journey our incredible contestants have taken… but all good things must come to an end at some point," the Gamemaster declared. "Fifty million people tuned in across the globe. You all want to see how this will end. Well, wait no longer. Let the final game begin."

CHAPTER TWENTY-EIGHT

"**B**UT FIRST... I THINK THERE'S SOMEONE ELSE WHO deserves a round of applause. The lady of the hour... the woman who made all of this possible. You've seen her in the movies, on your TV screens, and now she's here with us. Our most successful saboteur. A true actress to the end. Not one person suspected you until it was too late! Come on up here... Yara Montague!"

As the room broke into applause, Yara cowered in the corner, but one of the guards grabbed her and took her up to the stage. The four prisoners on the stage stared as she made her way up, unable to believe that she was the one who had betrayed them. Brock searched for Olivia's gaze once again, his eyes filled with hurt. Olivia couldn't blame him. She had never seen it coming, but how could he ever have known that his childhood friend, his ex-lover, would ever do this to him? It was something neither of them would ever be able to forget.

Yara was brought up to the stage, and the Gamemaster grabbed her hand, thrusting it into the air as though in triumph. Olivia felt her stomach twist. This was wrong. So, so wrong. But the crowd was loving it. They loved *her*. That was when Olivia realized how sick the game had become. It was like they were characters in a TV show, not real people. How could these people stand in the same room as her and see her as less than human?

"Yara has just pulled off the most convincing performance of her career, don't you think?" the Gamemaster said. Olivia couldn't see their face behind their mask, but she knew they were grinning. "Hollywood might've washed her up like a plastic bag on a beach, but we all see the potential in her, don't we? And all while going through alcohol withdrawal… what a woman! First, she was a latecomer to the island while I… *persuaded* her to come onto my team. I promised her that I'd help her through her struggles if she worked for me. And so, we became a dynamic duo, didn't we Yara? You did everything I asked of you, and you did it so well. But you already know what my proudest moment was… when you picked up the gun and worked as an assassin for me. Poor Harry didn't know what hit him."

Olivia stared at Yara in horror. She was the assassin as well? Olivia had thought Yara was capable of the things she'd done to them… but she didn't see her as a killer. Yara was sobbing now, but no one could hear her over the sound of the crowd cheering. A tear slid down Olivia's cheek. This was her last straw.

Yara could never be redeemed now for what she'd done.

"I didn't want to," Yara sobbed. "I was dying… I did what I had to do to survive…"

Olivia shook her head. Would she do the same in Yara's shoes? If she was on death's door, would she be willing to betray everyone she loved? She hoped not. But the desperation in Yara's eyes made Olivia want to look away from her. She didn't want to feel sorry for her. Not after she'd killed Harry. Not when she had so much blood on her hands.

This whole time, Olivia had been fighting tooth and nail to save everyone around her. She had risked her life for each and every person on the island. But behind the scenes, Yara had been dead set on stopping her from succeeding. And maybe that would've been forgivable, if she hadn't ended Harry's life.

Now, she couldn't see past that.

"I'm so proud of my little prodigy," the Gamemaster crooned, rubbing the small of Yara's back. "Such a star in the making. And since you're now a wanted woman in America, I'll keep you at my side and keep you safe. You won't go to prison under my watch. Give it up for the lovely Yara Montague, everyone!"

The audience clapped one final time, and Olivia watched as Yara was escorted to the side of the room to be guarded by the Gamemaster's minions. Olivia was glad to have her out of sight. She didn't know if she would ever be able to look at Yara again and not feel stabbing pain in her heart. She recalled how only twenty-four hours ago, she was comforting her on the beach, making out like she was her friend when she was only twisting the knife deeper.

"But that's enough of that! It's time for the main event! The one you've all been waiting for!" the Gamemaster declared. "And boy, oh, boy, is this going to be good. Olivia, if you'd be so kind as to join me up front…"

Olivia felt a gun poke her in the back, and she knew she had no choice but to comply. She walked slowly toward the stage, her friends looking terrified before her. She hated leaving Melody behind, too, but she hoped that would mean she was safe.

"As our fan favorite contestant, you have a very special task assigned to you," the Gamemaster told her. "Before your eyes sit the four leftover contestants who didn't make it into the top two. One of them will carry out the final task for the rest. And just so that it's fair for you, I'm going to tell you what it is… whoever you choose will fight to the death with our very special guest. I'm sure you're *dying* to know who that is, but that would be a spoiler, and we don't like those here!"

The crowd laughed wildly and cheered. Olivia felt sick. How was she supposed to pick someone and throw them into such a dangerous situation? Her eyes scanned the four people in front of her. Terror was rooted deep in them all, even Brock. How could it not be? For all they knew, the special guest was going to kill them within seconds. It was all too much.

But Olivia knew that there was only one choice. Only one of them would stand a chance in a battle. The twins weren't built to fight, and Henry was still learning how to stand on his new legs. He was in no shape to fight like he was before. And that left Brock. And everyone in that room knew it.

"I'll give you a few minutes to decide," the Gamemaster said, sounding amused. "Perhaps the audience will have some ideas of who you should pick?"

The audience began to shout their preferences of who they thought should be thrown into the battle. One name rose above the rest. "*Brock! Brock! Brock!*"

Olivia wanted nothing more than to sink to her knees and cover her ears to make it all stop. This was sickening. It was wrong. But that didn't mean she didn't have a decision to make.

Her eyes latched on to Brock's. There was pain in his eyes like never before. This is what he'd predicted. That somehow, one of them would die before they could make it home—almost as though this whole thing was built just for the two of them—to make sure at least one of them was eliminated. Was it Eve hiding behind the Gamemaster's mask, gleefully waiting to watch one of them die at her hand?

But Olivia knew that Brock was going to have to fight. He knew it too. He nodded to her solemnly. He understood the choice she had to make. If the tables were turned, she would understand too. They were both powerhouses. Olivia could only pray that whoever Brock would go up against was no match for him. That he could finish the horrible business and then maybe they'd be free to go.

"I choose Brock," Olivia said quietly.

"I can't hear you, Olivia," the Gamemaster teased, though it was clear who Olivia had chosen. She tilted her chin up and glared at the Gamemaster.

"Brock will fight. And he'll win," she said defiantly. The Gamemaster chuckled.

"Oh, are you so sure about that? You haven't met our other champion yet," the Gamemaster reminded her. "And I think things are going to get a lot more interesting when you see who I've brought in for this special occasion."

Olivia's hands curled into fists. The Gamemaster clearly thought they had the upper hand now. But what they didn't know was that Olivia was entirely willing to bend the rules in her favor. No one had said that she couldn't fight too. No one had said that she couldn't take down anyone who could possibly be on the other side. And since everyone in the room seemed so determined to be entertained, she'd make sure she put on a show. They would all pay for what they'd done to her and her friends.

Several guards came to the stage to untie Brock and free the others, escorting them from the stage. Olivia readied herself for anything, looking around the room for her starting point. The guards would likely try to stop her, but all she needed was to get her hands on a gun. Then the power would be in her hands. It was still her duty to protect innocents, and if she died trying, then so be it.

"The rules are simple. Fight until someone is dead," the Gamemaster said smoothly. "If you stop or try to protest, I'll start killing everyone else I can get my hands on. So, you best be ready to fight, Brock. The lives of your friends are in your hands."

Brock nodded solemnly. He was ready to die for everyone else if he had to. But Olivia wasn't going to allow that to happen either. They were a team. And she wanted to be on the winning side.

"Bring out the special guest," the Gamemaster declared. Olivia watched as a man stumbled onto the stage with much protest, struggling against the guards who held him. And all of a sudden, Olivia's plans went straight to the back of her mind.

Because the special guest was none other than ASAC Jonathan James.

CHAPTER TWENTY-NINE

OLIVIA'S PLANS WERE IMMEDIATELY THROWN OFF WHEN she saw who Brock would be fighting. She had no idea how this had happened. What the hell was Jonathan doing there? The Gamemaster laughed at Olivia's expression. They had clearly been waiting to make this reveal for some time.

"I warned the FBI not to intervene," the Gamemaster said darkly. "Oh, but Jonathan. Stodgy, old, by-the-book Jonathan. You simply couldn't leave well enough alone, could you?"

"You'll pay for this," he grumbled, but the Gamemaster was unphased.

"Not before you do."

The comment sent a cold chill down Olivia's spine, and Jonathan stopped struggling. The Gamemaster laughed it off. "I couldn't allow his meddling to continue. So, I had him kidnapped and brought here. And now the FBI is all upside down trying to figure out what to do. Isn't that hilarious?"

Jonathan was a mess. He was so different from his typical, buttoned-up self. His hair was unruly, and he had several scuffs and scratches on his face, undoubtedly from struggling against his captors. But even still, he gathered himself and gave a meaningful look at Brock.

"Tanner," he said. All the emotion he ever needed was in that simple word.

"Jonathan," Brock replied, still standing gingerly on his wounded leg.

Olivia shook her head in disbelief. This couldn't be. The game had just changed again, and she couldn't keep up with everything the Gamemaster was throwing at them. Whoever they were, they were sick beyond belief.

"Anyway. Start fighting," the Gamemaster said, clapping their gloved hands together. "Or I'll start shooting."

Olivia's fury rose to the surface. She couldn't back down now. She had no doubt that the guards would start shooting at her the moment she moved, but she wasn't afraid of them. They were no match for her when she had so much to lose.

Brock and Jonathan were facing off, staring at one another in horror. Jonathan threw a light punch, a love tap really, at Brock's shoulder. The Gamemaster tutted.

"Not like that! Harder!"

Olivia took that as her cue to act. She set off at a run toward the Gamemaster. Immediately, the guards dotted around the room began to spring into action. Olivia barreled straight into the first one that challenged her, knocking him to the ground and throwing a punch into his throat. He gasped for air, and Olivia quickly disarmed him, grabbing his wrist, snapping it quickly, and wrenching his gun out of its holster. But before she could even bring the pistol to bear, someone grabbed her arm from behind, trying to detain her. She whirled around and slammed the gun into the man's face, hearing his jaw crack. Then she aimed her knee straight for his crotch, toppling him onto the ground in agony.

The Gamemaster seemed torn as to what to watch. Jonathan and Brock were wrestling now, starting to get the fight going for real. They had no other choice, after all. But the Gamemaster kept casting glances at Olivia as the guards began to swarm her. Clearly, she was just as entertaining.

But there were so many of them now. Olivia could barely breathe as the guards closed in on her. She took two more down with relative ease, but their bodies were pressing tighter around her, giving her no room to maneuver. She was going to be crushed before she had a chance to get to the Gamemaster.

That was when Olivia heard the feral cry coming from the outside of the circle. She briefly saw Melody atop a guard's back, her forearm pressed to the man's windpipe, before she toppled him over. Then, from another angle, she heard a feminine cry, and she knew Clementine and Elodie had joined the fray. Capitalizing on the confusion of the guards, Olivia swung her fist into the jaw of a guard. He was a big guy, and the surprise shot sent him toppling into several others like a bowling ball.

The room had erupted into chaos, but Olivia wasn't about to back down. She thrashed her way through the crowd until she could see her friends in full throttle, fighting back. The audience seemed to think that it was all a part of the performance, and none of them tried to interfere, enjoying every second of it. Henry grabbed one guard by the shoulder and shoved him into another, and all of a sudden, a path was cleared toward the Gamemaster, a chance Olivia wasn't about to miss. But as she was making a run for it, she heard Elodie cry out as she fell to the ground, a guard grabbing her by the throat. Olivia backtracked to rescue her, cracking the guard on the back of the head with her gun, not daring to risk firing in such a confined, crowded area. The guard fell limp atop Elodie, and Olivia hauled him off her, checking in on her friend before setting her sights back on the Gamemaster.

Brock and Jonathan were both looking a little beat-up now. Brock's nose was bleeding, and Jonathan was red in the face from exertion, but both were obviously holding back. Olivia knew that it wouldn't be long before the Gamemaster insisted on things becoming more violent. Olivia would never forgive herself if one of them died there.

It was time to take down the Gamemaster.

But the guards just kept coming. Olivia hadn't realized just how many there were in the room. Every time she took a few steps forward, she was forced to block off another guard and deal with them.

But there was someone making their way through the crowd, clumsily pushing and barreling through the guards. In the corner of her eye, Olivia saw how the woman was struggling to stay on her feet, but she still kept thrashing out, managing to make life a little harder for the guards, even if she couldn't quite take them down.

Yara.

Olivia swallowed. She was trying to redeem herself, if that was even possible. She didn't think she could just forget what she'd done. But she had given Olivia an opening, and she had to take it. She'd deal with her messy feelings later.

Olivia ran for the stage and leaped up on top of it. The Gamemaster turned to her, surprise evident even with their mask on, and Olivia slammed into them, toppling them to the ground.

"Everybody stop, or I'll kill the Gamemaster!" Olivia cried out wildly. The room seemed to fall deathly silent as she towered over the slight frame of the Gamemaster. They chuckled beneath her, seemingly unfazed by the fact that they had been taken down.

"Go ahead, Olivia. Unmask me. I know you want to," the Gamemaster whispered. The words sent a chill down her spine. Was it someone she knew? Was she dealing with Eve after all? Olivia's hands were shaking a little as she reached forward and tore away the Gamemaster's mask.

It wasn't Eve.

It was a teenage girl.

CHAPTER THIRTY

OLIVIA STARED DOWN AT THE YOUNG GIRL AS SHE laughed in Olivia's face, a manic look in her clear, blue eyes. Of all the things Olivia expected, the last thing she imagined was that their mastermind was a *child*. She couldn't be much older than eighteen, and yet she had done so many terrible things. Olivia felt sick looking at her, angelic blond curls falling around her shoulders. She had rosy cheeks that seemed to complete her doll-like look. It only made the whole thing seem even stranger.

The girl shoved Olivia off her and stood up to take a bow while the audience clapped for her. Olivia aimed her gun at the young woman, but the girl raised an eyebrow.

"Relax, Olivia. You got me," the girl said, tossing her microphone to one side to unveil her true voice. Her voice was sweet as sugar, and it was turning Olivia's stomach. "I'm just here to take my final bow. Can't a girl go out with a bang?"

Brock and Jonathan had stopped fighting, and both of them were brushing themselves off, blinking in shock at the scene before them. Meanwhile, the young woman was lapping up every second of her finale, bowing and blowing kisses to the crowd.

"Thank you, thank you all!" she said theatrically. "I guess it's finally time that I introduced myself to you all properly. My name is Adeline Clarke. You might know me as the daughter of the billionaires, Alexander and Sasha Clarke. Now some of you will know why you were invited. You were all members of their inner circle… before their untimely death not so long ago."

The crowd let out an *aww*, as if they hadn't just been gleefully grinning while innocent people fought to the death right in front of them. Olivia gripped her gun even harder. There was no telling what this strange, young woman might try next.

"I think the contestants may be curious as to why they're here too," Adeline continued. "Anyone recognize me?"

"It's you…" Melody said, staring at Adeline. "We met at that event in Prague six months ago. You… you told me to book a trip to the spa. You said you'd meet me there. We've… been texting for *six whole months*."

Adeline grinned at Melody. "I do like to commit to a bit. And I bet you remember me, don't you Elodie?"

Elodie blushed. "You took me on a date when I was in London for the weekend three months ago… we had… we had a wonderful night. You promised me you'd come to the spa retreat. You said to bring Clem… said you wanted to meet my sister."

Adeline laughed. "It really was a lovely date we had, Elodie. But as you've probably guessed, I did have ulterior motives. I wanted each of you to get on that plane that day. Apart from our dear Rose… who is safe, by the way, and in FBI protection. As Yara said… she was never meant to be there. Wrong place at the wrong time."

"Not me, though," Henry said through gritted teeth. "You sought me out. You made sure I got on that flight."

"Of course, I did. Because I needed you there. Just like Yara had to be there. It was easy enough to persuade her to go on a spa retreat to detox… it was all planned."

"Why this group of people? What did you hope to gain?" Olivia asked, narrowing her eyes. Adeline gestured around her.

"Look around you, Olivia Knight. You're surrounded by the rich and famous. I wanted to draw an audience. I wanted celebrities who were just off the radar enough that the world wouldn't be mad at me for putting them through so much. Some nice C-listers who wouldn't be in too much public demand to be here, right?"

The audience laughed, and Olivia saw Melody blush.

"What about Brock? Me? Henry?" Olivia pushed. Adeline smirked.

"Let's just say that we have some mutual acquaintances. My parents were filthy rich— which is exactly how I funded all of my livestreaming ventures, of course—but they kept bad company. Who do you think that was?"

"ANH," Olivia said without hesitation. Everything kept leading back to them. She'd been so sure that Eve Valentine was the one orchestrating this whole thing, and Adeline had even mentioned ANH when they spoke for the first time.

"Very good, Olivia. You're not such a bad detective after all, even if you did get bested by a nineteen-year-old. I found out about my parents funding ANH after I inherited their multibillion-dollar fortune. I had to sift through all these boring documents and try to make sense of it. But after a while, it got interesting. I was watching nine-figure sums disappear in each year's statements. I wanted to know where it was going. And of course, it was going straight into ANH's pocket. If you think I'm bad, imagine what my parents were willingly funding. At least my ventures have been entertaining the masses."

"I hardly think that makes up for what you've done," Olivia snarled. Adeline laughed.

"Oh, well. I guess I can live with that. I probably get that trait from my parents," she said. "Apple doesn't fall too far from the tree. Anyway, just before they died, they were trying to expand their bases. I looked into it. They planned to make moves in a nonextradition country… Saudi Arabia, I believe it was. My father had always had connections there. But they never got that far. You see… they were in a plane crash of their own. On the very island that you became so familiar with over this last week. Except they weren't given a chance. There were no parachutes for them. Everyone on the plane died. They were on their way to do business in Saudi Arabia, so I guess I blame ANH for getting my parents roped in. Their greed killed them. And now I'm on my own. Fortunately, the FBI never traced the ANH funding back to me and mine. Just goes to show how incompetent you all are." Adeline paused to sigh. "Life was tough after that. I dropped out of college and came back home. Can I get an aww?"

The audience obeyed her and made a sympathetic sound. Adeline stuck out her bottom lip and motioned crying theatrically. Olivia rolled her eyes. Adeline might not be Eve, but she was certainly on a similar level to her.

"So, I did what any sane, grieving daughter would do. I bought the island for myself and decided to have a little fun with it. It's not every day you get to move people around like puppets, you know. Little marionettes twirling, twirling, twirling on strings." She lifted a finger and moved it in a circle, the happy memories floating on her face as she reminisced.

"Anyway, as you figured out already, there were other contestants that came before you. Just some dumb assholes who said they were willing to try it out with a cash prize as a reward. Some of them walked away with a stupid amount of money. Some weren't so lucky."

"You're a monster."

"Oh, well. I'm having fun," she grinned. "But I have to say, you all surprised me. You survived much better than I thought you would. Mostly thanks to Olivia, but still, it was impressive. You all deserve to walk away with your lives. And you will. My word is good."

Olivia's mouth dropped open. "And how are we supposed to trust that?"

"Oh, please. The FBI is already on its way to pick up the pieces of this mess. I never planned to get out of this one. I've had my fun, but I think it's time for me to retire. Prison will probably be a nice change of pace for me. But that's the nature of the game. I've really enjoyed every second of this. Maybe someday you'll have a sense of humor about all of this."

"Don't count on it," Brock snarled.

Adeline winked at Olivia. "He's a keeper, Olivia. All the viewers have been rooting for your little love story. He's very macho, isn't he?"

Olivia heard footsteps coming from outside the ballroom. It had to be the FBI agents taking the boat back. Adeline scanned the crowd one final time, bowing for them all.

"Thank you, thank you, thank you. I've been your host, Adeline Clarke. If you've enjoyed my little show, don't forget to like, share, and subscribe! I'll be going dark for a while, but don't worry. I will be back."

The doors to the ballroom burst open, and FBI agents spilled in pointing their guns around at the guards and guests. Adeline sighed and began to walk toward them, her hands raised.

"Don't worry; I'll come quietly," she said with a sweet smile. "Oh, and I want my watchers to know… all of the money made from my streams is going straight to charity! Don't say I don't do anything nice for you…"

And with that, Olivia could see it was over. She ran to Brock and Jonathan's aid, checking them over. They were bruised and battered, but they'd live. They all would. After everything they'd gone through, that was something, at least.

They were finally going home.

CHAPTER THIRTY-ONE

Stepping off the plane to flashing cameras was enough to make Olivia feel sick to her stomach—as though they hadn't already been gobbled up by enough cameras to last a lifetime. She pulled her hood up over her head and stuck her hands in her pockets, stalking past the lines of paparazzi and to the black car that awaited them. They were headed straight to a media conference where they'd address everything they'd been through with the Gamemaster.

It still hadn't quite sunk in what they'd all been put through and who was behind it all. Olivia had dealt with some scary cases, but this had to be one of the worst. It was hard to feel like they'd truly escaped; in some ways, it felt like they were still stuck in the thick of it all looking for a way out.

As she clambered into the car, she was followed by Jonathan, Henry, Brock, and Melody. Clementine and Elodie had flown straight home to France after their brief stint in the hospital, not interested in telling their story to crowds of hungry journalists. Olivia and Brock were left with no choice but to address everything, and Jonathan, of course, wanted to make a statement as well. Yara, for obvious reasons, wasn't with them.

As they drove to the conference, Yara was on Olivia's mind. She didn't know how to feel about her. After everything she had done, she didn't feel redeemable in Olivia's eyes. But she couldn't put herself in Yara's shoes. She had been a desperate woman. She likely would've died without the Gamemaster's help. And yes, she did kill one of her own, but she was terrified for her life. Could Olivia forgive that?

Brock felt for her hand in the car, and Olivia closed her eyes. She knew he had to be turning the thought over in his mind too. Yara had been his friend for such a long time. Had he ever imagined that she was capable of betraying him so terribly? That she would be willing to trade someone else's life to save her own? Olivia hadn't known Harry well, but she knew that had the tables been turned, she wouldn't have killed him. She would've done whatever she could to protect him. And that was the difference between her and Yara. That was the reason Yara was headed straight to prison, and the rest of them were leaving the island without blood on their hands.

It could've been so much worse. They had seen terrible things: one accidental death, one suicide, one murder, and one death for not following the rules. But they could've easily turned on each other. They could've all gone to dark places inside themselves to protect their own backs. But for the most part, the people Olivia had met on the island had stayed good people. She opened her eyes and glanced at Melody. She'd been quiet since the fight on the cruise liner, and she looked like she hadn't slept in days. But Olivia thought about everything she'd persevered through and felt proud of the young girl.

She had started so nervous, so fearful of what would become of them. But she had grown. She had proved herself to the others, and most importantly, to herself. It was that spirit, that strength, that kept the group together. She'd even saved Olivia's life from David's betrayal. That was something to hold on to. Even if nightmares of that island haunted them forever, Olivia would always remember the young girl who fought by her side the entire time.

"Who wants to lead the speeches?" Henry said after a long silence. "I certainly bloody don't."

Olivia allowed a small smile. At least her grumpy British friend never truly changed.

"I don't mind speaking on everyone's behalf," Olivia said. Brock squeezed her hand.

"Yes. It really should be you," he said with a decisive nod. "I don't think we'd have made it through without you."

"You should see all the articles about you," Melody said, her face glued to her phone. She was scrolling through endless websites that were talking about the whole debacle. "They're calling you a hero. And some of these old cases they've brought to light… it's no wonder. You took down an entire criminal organization that was running for over twenty years? You fought a mass murderer at a waterfall? And you were the one who caught Landon Brown's killer? Do you ever take a day off?"

"No, she doesn't," Brock said with a knowing wink at Olivia. She smirked, dipping her head as she recalled their disastrous skiing trip. "But one thing's for sure. I'm not desperate for any sort of desert island retreat anytime soon."

The group laughed as they pulled up in front of FBI headquarters. Only then did Olivia's stomach twist with nerves. She didn't really want to face this today. She wanted nothing more than to go back home to Belle Grove and sleep for a few days. Or months. She had barely recovered from Landon's case when they'd been swept off to the island.

But she knew she couldn't hide away from this. The whole world had watched as they were ferried off to survive the Gamemaster's sick games. Now, Adeline was headed straight for prison along with Yara and her other cronies. People would want to hear about what happened, and Olivia was more inclined to tell her own version than let anyone else tell it for her. She knew all too well how narratives could be twisted, how everyone could see what the Gamemaster had wanted them to see. She had to tell the truth. They'd lived through it; they'd suffered unimaginable things. No one could talk about it better than they could.

As they exited the car, more cameras and journalists bombarded them. These ones at least seemed to have some respect, and they politely waited as the group filed in to city hall to make their statements.

Inside, a familiar face was waiting for them. Olivia's face split into a wide, genuine grin as she caught sight of Rose standing nervously off to one side of the room. She burst into tears as they all moved to greet her, enveloping her in a gentle hug.

"Thank goodness you're all okay," Rose sobbed. "I felt so guilty for leaving you all there…"

"Don't be ridiculous, Rose. It's all right," Melody soothed her gently, cupping her cheek. "Are you all right? What happened with you?"

Rose swallowed back her tears. "The Gamemaster greeted me on a boat and took me off the island. She… she explained that she never intended for me to get involved. I really was in the wrong place at the wrong time. She… she offered to give me a million dollars to start up a new life, to cover the emotional damages she did to me and my child… but I couldn't take such an offer. Not when I knew there had to be a catch. When I knew the money had come from somewhere horrible. I knew that wasn't the way I wanted my child to grow up. I didn't want them to become like… well, like the Gamemaster. Money doesn't solve everything, right?"

"It doesn't," Olivia agreed. "Though no one would have blamed you for taking the offer. Not after everything we went through."

"Some things are more important than money. I don't need it to give my child a good life," Rose whispered. "And I don't want this hanging over my head for their whole life. After today… well… I want to try to forget about it entirely."

Olivia wondered if it was worth telling Rose that it would be impossible to forget what they went through. She didn't want to scare her or make her feel bad, but it was true. Life would never be the same for any of them again. There was only so much of it that they could shove to the back of their minds. Olivia had spent the entire plane ride dreaming of every terrible possibility she might have to rerun. She knew she'd have a tough time ever getting on a plane again, or seeing snakes and scorpions, or even watching reality TV.

The Gamemaster had put a mark on her life that she'd never be able to get rid of. And now, it was time to let the world know what a monster the young girl really was. It was time to show them all that what they'd been through should never have been treated as entertainment. She hoped that her speech might get through to some people. There would always be those who remembered the Gamemaster's little experiment with awe and wonder, but Olivia thought that was shameful. How could so much death bring entertainment?

The hall was getting busier, and Olivia was ushered to the front of the room with her fellow contestants and Jonathan. Brock put a hand on the small of her back.

"Are you sure you're ready to do this? You don't have to if you don't feel ready," he murmured to her. Olivia looked at his bruised face and his swollen ankle, and sadness swelled in her heart. He had been through even more than she had. How would he ever forget fist-fighting his boss for the entertainment of rich folks, knowing that one of them was supposed to wind up dead by the end of the fight? How would he ever move past the fact that his friend had been the reason so many of them suffered? She had to do this speech for him, if not for herself. She cupped his swollen cheek gently.

"I can do this," she murmured. "I have to do this."

When Olivia stepped up to the podium to speak, the room fell into an uncomfortable silence. Olivia looked around the room and wondered how many of the people there had watched the games. Had they resisted the temptation, or had they tuned in every day in excitement? Nothing so awful had ever happened live before for the world to watch. She imagined that morbid curiosity would get the better of many of them. She didn't like to believe it, but it was a part of history now. Who could turn away from that?

"I stand here today as the mouthpiece of the survivors of the island," Olivia began slowly. "Our worlds were turned upside down last week when the Gamemaster deliberately crashed us into a desert island with the sole intention of making our lives hell. Why? To entertain herself and the world. Adeline Clarke was born into an evil family—a family who funded organizations such as ANH with no guilt in their hearts. Adeline took what her parents taught her and put it into practice, thus destroying lives all around her in her wake. I know that many people watched what happened to us and thought it was exciting, that it was funny, that it was the craziest thing they'd ever seen. But above that… I need the world to know just how horrifying it was. As an FBI agent, I've seen many things in my career… but nothing like this. This horrible experience will stay with me for a long, long time."

Olivia swallowed down the lump in her throat, keeping her eyes lowered to the podium. She was gripping it hard as she spoke, as if it were keeping her grounded. She knew it would be hard to talk about, but not this hard. She never expected the whole thing to impact her so deeply. But it was a struggle to voice the thoughts she'd been having over the past week.

"I want you all to remember the people we lost. Clive on the very first day—a man who didn't understand what he had been thrown into. And then there was Tess… a victim of the environment we were subjected to. Harry died at the hand of another contestant, someone who had been forced into that situation or risk death herself. David died because he couldn't live with the things he'd done. And those of us who survived have been left with experiences we will never forget. When you think of the days you spent watching us suffer on the island… think of Rose and her precious child growing inside her. Think of Henry, already a victim of unthinkable horrors. Think of Clementine and Elodie, two women just wanting to get to a spa retreat before their lives were ruined. And think of Melody, a woman forced to become a fighter just to survive. The changes we went through on that island were against our will. They will haunt us forever. Those were real lives affected by the Gamemaster and her plans. Don't forget that. Don't forget that even though we survived, it came at a great price to us all."

Olivia took a deep breath and stared out at the crowd. "And don't forget that all games have a loser… but this one certainly didn't have a winner."

With that, Olivia turned away from the podium. A million questions were being shouted at her, but she didn't want to hear them. She was done with the media circus, with these people trying to open the window into their lives even farther. They had been thrust into the spotlight against their will, but now, it was time to walk away.

It was time for them to go home.

CHAPTER THIRTY-TWO

It was an emotional moment when Olivia and Brock said goodbye to their new friends from the island. Henry was due to fly straight back to England, and Olivia wasn't quite ready to see him go. Olivia hugged him hard as his taxi waited to take him there.

"You keep in touch, okay?" she told him. He patted her back affectionately.

"Don't get too soppy with me, American. That's not how we do things."

"I think we can make an exception this time…"

"All right, all right. I'll see you soon, okay? And don't you be worrying about me. I think if I can survive that bloody island, then I must truly be invincible."

After he had left, it was time to say goodbye to Melody and Rose. Rose was red-cheeked as she leaned in to kiss both Brock and Olivia on the cheeks.

"I owe you both everything," she said gently. "I would love it if you would come and see me after the baby is born… perhaps you can help me think of a name for my little angel. You, too, Melody."

"We'd like that," Olivia said with a warm smile. Rose grasped her hand with love in her eyes.

"Seriously. Thank you. For everything. I hope that wherever your path takes you… it's somewhere better than where we've just been."

"Me, too, Rose. Me too."

Melody and Olivia waved as Rose's taxi took her away. Then there were only three of them. Melody turned to Olivia with tears in her eyes.

"Well. It's been quite a journey."

Olivia nodded, her throat tight. "It has."

"I've learned a lot from you, Olivia. And I'm glad that I wasn't on my own through all of this… you kept me strong. I will never ever forget how you got me through this ordeal. Any time you're in New York… please come and see me. I'd love to see you."

"We'll have to come and see you at one of your fashion shows. Or maybe even your law school graduation," Olivia said with a smile, but she knew that it was unlikely they'd cross paths anytime soon. Olivia knew better than most that her face only brought up bad memories. It was the curse of her job. She was always associated with the work she'd done. She might save lives, but she also only showed up during times of tragedy. That was something people couldn't forget in a hurry.

"Hey, I'm serious, you know. I'm not just saying it. I want to see you again. Don't go dark on me," Melody said, looking right into Olivia's eyes. A tear slipped from her eye. She had always struggled with keeping friends in her adulthood. It felt nice that someone was actively making an effort to remain in her life. Melody's friendship might be a product of their trauma, but if anything, maybe that made it more real.

The two women hugged hard, and Olivia found herself clinging tightly to her new friend. It was starting to feel impossible to let go. Those six intense days on the island had really formed a bond between them that she wouldn't forget in a hurry. And as much as Melody thought Olivia saved her, it worked both ways: Melody had saved Olivia too.

"This is silly. As if we're crying over goodbyes," Melody laughed, pulling away and wiping tears from her eyes. "After all we've been through, this is the part that breaks us, huh?"

Olivia laughed and sniffed, shaking her head. "You're right. It's silly. Get home safe, Melody. I'll see you around."

"You will, I promise," Melody said. She pulled Brock in for a quick hug. "Look after my girl, okay? She's tough, but a little love does her good, doesn't it?"

"Don't you worry. I'll watch her back," Brock said with a smile. Melody took a deep breath, backtracking several steps with a tight smile.

"All right. I'm going. Don't be strangers."

Olivia waved Melody off, fighting off the urge to cry once again. Brock put an arm around her, knowing she needed it at that moment. He kissed the top of her head lovingly.

"Come on. Let's get you out of here," Brock said. "We could both use a good night's rest, huh?"

After the exhausting flight and the press conference, neither Olivia nor Brock felt like driving straight back to Belle Grove. Olivia wanted everything to be normal again, and yet heading straight back to reality felt too hard after the week they'd had. She was glad when Brock insisted that they check in at a nice hotel in downtown DC, and then they spent the evening calling their loved ones and ordering an obscene amount of room service food. It gave her a welcome distraction to keep her busy.

"Oh, God. I've never felt so full in my life. And that's saying something," Brock said as he polished off his mountain of chicken wings. Olivia sat back on their hotel bed with a sigh, full from her Caesar salad and fries combo. It felt good to eat something other than protein bars, even though it had only been a week that they'd lived on canned goods and rationed portions. It was amazing to her how quickly the real world had faded away for her… and how hard it hit when she returned to it.

"I just can't believe we're here," she said. It was the simple things she had missed. She had spent over half an hour in the shower when they arrived at the hotel, just letting the hot water run over her dirty hair and her aching muscles. She couldn't remember a time when it had felt so good to just have basic things. For the first time in days, the uncomfortable feeling of sand under her nails and in between her toes was gone. She'd finally washed the smell of the sea out of her hair, and she'd almost burst into tears when she smelled the hotel's soap.

"Never again," Brock said, taking Olivia's hand. She closed her eyes. She knew what he meant. She hadn't forgotten what he had said to her before they got on the plane and accepted their fate at the island. He didn't want them to work together any longer. Now he was putting the final nail in the coffin. Olivia had understood what he meant right away, because working together was hard. But she never expected that he'd commit to what he'd said.

She didn't want it to end.

"Brock… don't do this," Olivia whispered to him. He turned to her with a frown, his brow furrowed.

"Do what?"

"I know you don't want to work together anymore. I know you think it's too dangerous for us, after everything we've been through together. I know our time on the island didn't help. But Brock… it only further proved to me that you're one of the few people on this planet that I can trust. After what happened with Yara… I just know that I need you to have my back, more than ever. How can I count on that if we're not working side by side? I'm not sure you're thinking through all we'd lose if we stopped being partners. I just… I can't bear the idea of you working with anyone other than me. I used to be okay working alone, and then you changed that. Don't leave me now, Brock. I need you more than ever."

Brock reached out to cup Olivia's cheek. She didn't realize she'd been crying until his thumb brushed away her tears.

"I don't want to stop working together anymore," he murmured. She blinked in shock.

"You… you don't?"

"No. I had an epiphany," Brock said with a slight smile. "When we were separated on the island… when you went off with Yara and Melody… I thought it was fine. Until we were captured. And that's when I began to think, *How would I get out of that situation without you? Who would be watching my back? And how could I watch yours if you were away from me?* It scared me half to death, Olivia. Because the thing is, we're a team now. We don't function the same when we're apart. And I know that you'd be okay without me. You might not be happy about it, but you'd survive, like you always do. But I don't think I could do any of this without you."

Olivia's expression softened. "That's not true."

"I hate to admit it, but it is. Do you remember how I was when we first met, Olivia? I'd stopped caring enough about the work. I was bored with my life; I was living life at the bare minimum. I was putting on a front for everyone, but on the inside, I was barely a person. You showed me how to be passionate again. You reminded me why I went into this line of work in the first place. And if I stop working with you, then where will I get my passion from? Because it's you that fuels it. It's always been you."

Olivia's heart ached. She had no idea Brock felt so strongly about the bond they had together at work. The love they shared for one another was a different thing entirely. But she had always thought that the work they did together was something he could take or leave. They clashed on almost everything when they were working a case—two headstrong characters with opposing ways of approaching everything.

But now she could see that it was the reason they worked so well together. They challenged one another, shaped one another's opinions, learned from each other. They made each other better. Olivia was so worried about losing her best friend that she hadn't thought as much about what she would lose in a partner. He was her perfect match both in the field and at home.

That was something neither of them could afford to lose.

"You really mean it? You don't want to stop working together?" Olivia asked gently. Brock nodded decisively.

"I'm certain. And I won't doubt it again. We will have challenges, for sure. But we will anyway. I would rather face them at your side than apart. And you're right. We can only truly rely on each other."

Olivia swallowed and held his hands hard. "I'm… I'm so sorry about Yara."

Brock bowed his head. "Me too. I never… well, I never would have seen that coming. But I don't think she ever could have predicted her path in life either. I don't think she's a bad person. Selfish, yes. Self-centered, yes. Kind of always has been, in a certain way. But that was what made her vulnerable—made her the perfect target for the Gamemaster to twist to her every whim. I don't blame her for what she did—not directly. That doesn't mean I forgive her either. But what she did is, well… she did what she thought she had to do to get out of there alive. I wouldn't have done that if I were in her position. Not to save my own life. But to save yours…?"

Olivia looked away. "You wouldn't."

"I don't know. I'm just glad that I wasn't placed in that situation," he clarified. "But that's the thing in our line of work. You realize you don't have to be truly evil to end someone's life. You just have to care more about yourself than the person you're pointing the gun at."

Olivia nodded again. Her throat was sore from being on the verge of tears. But somehow, they'd both survived. They'd saved so many people. Things could be so much worse. And yet they both had things to grieve that they never expected to. And the loss of Yara as a friend would long stay with them both.

"I'll miss her so much," Brock said, shaking his head. "But I can never forgive her. You're all I have left."

Olivia was quick to wrap Brock inside her arms, squeezing him hard. When he was honest, it was brutally so. She could feel Brock's loneliness radiating from him, and she held him even tighter. This was going to be a tough wound to heal.

But they'd do it together.

CHAPTER THIRTY-THREE

O LIVIA WAS GIVEN TWO WHOLE WEEKS OF PEACE BEFORE her world came crashing down around her again. She had no preparation, no way of seeing it coming. She had been on edge for a while, still working through the nightmares of what had happened on the island, but the morning before she received the news, everything seemed good.

She and Brock were preparing to head up to Washington for a debrief on a quick case they'd worked since they'd been home. It was the first time they were seeing Jonathan since the entire debacle, and Brock was putting off leaving.

"I mean, it's not going to be easy to forget that I almost broke his nose two weeks ago," Brock said as Olivia was packing up her bag for the day. "What am I supposed to say to him? Hey, boss, you're looking good today... considering that we beat the hell out of each other two weeks back."

"I think he'll have a sense of humor about the whole thing."

"Olivia, have you ever met the man? I don't think he's even capable of smiling. He physically doesn't have the capability."

"Well, maybe that's all changed now, ever since you rearranged his features..."

Brock spluttered out a laugh, and Olivia offered him a devilish smile. It was almost starting to feel like they could joke about what had happened. That was another thing she loved about her partnership with Brock. They did have a tendency to find opportunities for dark humor where they shouldn't.

"Man, Olivia, he definitely wouldn't like that joke," Brock laughed, heading for the door. "But I guess we'd better get this over and done with..."

But Olivia and Brock never got an opportunity to make any jokes, dark or otherwise. When they arrived at Jonathan's office, he stood immediately.

"Both of you need to sit down. I've just received some disturbing news."

Olivia and Brock exchanged a glance before sitting down solemnly. Jonathan leaned against the desk as he stood, looking unsteady on his feet.

"I'm getting far too old for this," he muttered. Then he glanced at the two agents in front of him. "You know that Adeline Clarke was due to be extradited to Interpol?"

Olivia nodded. She hadn't been told about when the transfer would be, just that it would be soon. She hadn't asked much about it. She didn't have any desire to know about where the Gamemaster was going to be held. But Olivia got the feeling that it was about to become her problem.

Jonathan pinched the bridge of his nose. "Well, the transfer was going to happen today. It was a very well-guarded transfer van... but something went wrong. There was a garbage truck that blocked off the entire road to the airport. It caused quite the collision on the main road. And then... four cars showed up and blocked the SUV in. Masked gunmen came out. They must have found out about the special cargo inside the van. They shot dead all the officers on duty. And now…"

"Adeline has escaped," Olivia finished for Jonathan. His face turned dark.

"Not just Adeline. Yara too."

AUTHOR'S NOTE

Thank you for reading *Fatal Games,* the tenth book in the *Olivia Knight FBI Series*. We genuinely hope that you were captivated by the high-stakes survival scenario that Olivia and Brock found themselves thrown into. But you know what made this book truly special for us? Crafting a situation that pushed Olivia and Brock to depend on each other like never before and exploring the unique dynamics among the survivors. We are eager to hear your thoughts on how we did!

Our goal remains to provide you with the perfect escape into a world of non-stop excitement and action with every book. However, we can't do it alone! As indie writers, we don't have a big marketing budget or a massive following to help spread the word. That's where you come in! If you love the Olivia Knight series, please take a moment to leave us a review and tell your fellow book lovers about our latest installment. With your help, we can continue to bring you more thrilling adventures with Olivia and Brock, and make our mark in the world of crime fiction.

Thank you for your continued support, and we can't wait to take you on more thrilling adventures with the *Olivia Knight FBI* series!

By the way, if you find any typos, have suggestions, or just simply want to reach out to us, feel free to email us at egray@ellegraybooks.com

Your writer friends,
Elle Gray & K.S. Gray

CONNECT WITH ELLE GRAY

Loved the book? Don't miss out on future reads! Join my newsletter and receive updates on my latest releases, insider content, and exclusive promos. Plus, as a thank you for joining, you'll get a FREE copy of my book Deadly Pursuit!

Deadly Pursuit follows the story of Paxton Arrington, a police officer in Seattle who uncovers corruption within his own precinct. With his career and reputation on the line, he enlists the help of his FBI friend Blake Wilder to bring down the corrupt Strike Team. But the stakes are high, and Paxton must decide whether he's willing to risk everything to do the right thing.

Claiming your freebie is easy! Visit
https://dl.bookfunnel.com/513mluk159
and sign up with your email!

Want more ways to stay connected? Follow me on Facebook and Instagram or sign up for text notifications by texting "blake" to 844-552-1368. Thanks for your support and happy reading!

ALSO BY
ELLE GRAY

Blake Wilder FBI Mystery Thrillers

Book One - The 7 She Saw
Book Two - A Perfect Wife
Book Three - Her Perfect Crime
Book Four - The Chosen Girls
Book Five - The Secret She Kept
Book Six - The Lost Girls
Book Seven - The Lost Sister
Book Eight - The Missing Woman
Book Nine - Night at the Asylum
Book Ten - A Time to Die
Book Eleven - The House on the Hill
Book Twelve - The Missing Girls
Book Thirteen - No More Lies
Book Fourteen - The Unlucky Girl
Book Fifteen - The Heist
Book Sixteen - The Hit List
Book Seventeen - The Missing Daughter
Book Eighteen - The Silent Threat

A Pax Arrington Mystery
Free Prequel - Deadly Pursuit
Book One - I See You
Book Two - Her Last Call
Book Three - Woman In The Water
Book Four - A Wife's Secret

Storyville FBI Mystery Thrillers
Book One - The Chosen Girl
Book Two - The Murder in the Mist

A Sweetwater Falls Mystery
Book One - New Girl in the Falls
Book Two - Missing in the Falls
Book Three - The Girls in the Falls

ALSO BY
ELLE GRAY | K.S. GRAY

Olivia Knight FBI Mystery Thrillers
Book One - New Girl in Town
Book Two - The Murders on Beacon Hill
Book Three - The Woman Behind the Door
Book Four - Love, Lies, and Suicide
Book Five - Murder on the Astoria
Book Six - The Locked Box
Book Seven - The Good Daughter
Book Eight - The Perfect Getaway
Book Nine - Behind Closed Doors
Book Ten - Fatal Games

ALSO BY
ELLE GRAY | JAMES HOLT

The Florida Girl FBI Mystery Thrillers
Book One - The Florida Girl

Printed in Great Britain
by Amazon